Head in the Heavens
An Anthology

E.B. Dawson

Copyright © 2019 by **E.B. Dawson**

All rights reserved. No part of this publication may be reproduced, distributed or transmitted in any form or by any means, without prior written permission.

E.B. Dawson
www.ebdawsonwriting.com

Publisher's Note: This is a work of fiction. Names, characters, places, and incidents are a product of the author's imagination. Locales and public names are sometimes used for atmospheric purposes. Any resemblance to actual people, living or dead, or to businesses, companies, events, institutions, or locales is completely coincidental.

Book Layout © 2019 BookDesignTemplates.com

Head in the Heavens/ E.B. Dawson. -- 1st ed.
ISBN 9781393163305

CPSIA information can be obtained
at www.ICGtesting.com
Printed in the USA
LVHW111510181019
634647LV00002B/358/P

For Shyla
Who has been waiting so patiently
For this anthology

TABLE OF CONTENTS

NOMAD OF THE EMIRATES 1

GOVERNMENT MAN 31
    THE CONTACT 32
    TOMORROW 38
    ABOUT THREE WEEKS LATER 46
    NOT DEAD 52
    FUGITIVE 60

SHADOW FIGURE 69
    CAPTURED 70
    CONVERSATIONS 75
    FLIGHT 82
    THE SHADOW FIGURE 86
    TURNING POINT 90

GIFTED 99
    UNDERGROUND 100
    THE ALBINO 104
    THE CHAMPION 109
    THE FIGHT 114
    AGAINST ALL ODDS 121
    THE STORM 125
    QUESTIONS 130
    GIFTED 134

BEAST IN THE MACHINE 142

VOYAGE OF THE PEQUOD 204

NOMAD OF THE EMIRATES

I first saw the woman from Earth on Harvest Day, or as we non-Imperial citizens like to call it, "Gleaning Day." She was tall and square, perfectly toned, and clearly military. You could tell from her uniform but it was even more obvious in her face and body language. I thought she must have been bred for the position like a thoroughbred racehorse. And it was clear why her government had chosen her as envoy to the Emirates—her keen eyes pierced everything they set their sights on, filtered by the weight of those indomitable, military-trained eyebrows. Even from my distance I could see that those eyebrows were working overtime to cast away or reinterpret the cacophony of alien information assaulting her from every side. This one might not have a panic attack.

She stood beside the Shah and his chieftains on the hovering platform, receiving the refreshments that were thrust upon her with a stern courtesy. Even at this distance I could see her uniform—once crisply pressed—wilting under the blistering sun, but she stood tall and dignified as the Shah explained to her the process of harvest transfer.

The enormous Collector had descended to its target altitude, five hundred meters above the stubble fields with their odd contours of luminescent magenta, and cast a shadow the size of a football field. Dozens of Harvesters had lined up in half a dozen parallel queues and began sliding forward across the fumes of boiling air churned up by their ventilators.

To the untrained eye, it looked like a procession of tanks marching off to war, and I wondered briefly if the Earth woman would understand it. But when each Harvester slid under the belly of the monster Collector, the transfer of Perillian Grain was unmistakable. The harvest load was propelled upward with a shocking amount of force and speed almost invisible to the naked eye aside from the cloud of gold and magenta dust which was produced. It was from this cloud that the rain came—a warm, earthy, nutritious rain of magenta tipped stalks. It was for this life-giving rain that I had come—I along with about seven thousand others.

You may think it far-fetched that she would spot me in all that crowd, moving back and forth like the waves of the ocean under the belly of machines. But as soon as I saw her, I knew she would. Anyone who's traveled abroad knows how remarkably easy it is to pick out a fellow countryman. My skin had tanned, but its smooth quality practically glowed next to the rough, textured patterns of any given Emiratee. My dark brown hair stood out like a weed among their naturally ethereal silver manes. I hadn't planned on causing a scene. But those heavy-filter eyebrows, so determined to keep her own understanding of the world safe inside, proved irresistible.

Her gaze fell on me, but her expression didn't change. I could almost see her considering the possibility that I was simply a mutant Emiratee. I decided to clarify the matter for her with an impromptu performance of "Single Ladies" that would have brought the house down in my non-English speaking karaoke club back home. But when I looked back at the platform she had vanished. The Emiratees had ignored my antics, accustomed to my peculiarities and much more concerned with getting their winter store of Perillian grain. But now they suddenly stirred and parted and I caught sight of a very red-faced Captain hurtling toward me. I panicked and ran.

Now, I'm no couch potato. I like to think I'm the spoon in the silverware drawer of athletics. I really only have one area of expertise, and I'm a little round in some places, but I can substitute for a fork or a knife if I have to. Unfortunately running is *not* my area of expertise and the furious female Captain with the indomitable eyebrows tackled me in under a minute. I do pride myself on being scrappy. But pit scrappy, Spoon-Girl against thoroughbred Fighting Machine with a point to prove and you get a pretty pathetic picture. I didn't imagine she'd put me in a chokehold. I guess I need to expand my imagination. And she didn't let up when I tapped out—not until I had nearly blacked out.

Well, I had *majorly* misjudged that situation. You live and you learn. But now she was hauling me to my feet as the ground tilted dementedly and the brown-cloth shoes of the Emiratees around us blinked in and out of focus. Before I knew what was happening my hands had been bound with a rough cord and I had been dragged into a small transport. The world had stopped vomiting at me and it was time to assess the gravity of my situation. My fellow earthling sat across from me looking very angry. I wanted water. I could ask for it, but in her present mood she was likely to water-board me. Luckily, she spoke first.

"How did you get here?"

"Umm...I ran into a merchant a couple years ago." I suddenly thought this information might put those eyebrows over the edge. "The Emiratees have been watching Earth for about ten years now."

"I know that," she snapped. She swallowed hard. "They've been making contact with Americans?"

"Earth products are in high demand: silk, chili powder, scented candles… The merchants have become pretty good at blending in."

Through the transport windows I could just see ripe fields flashing by, occasionally accented by dark soil and scraggly trees.

Her jaw contracted. I hadn't thought she could get any angrier. My imagination really is pretty limited, I guess.

"Where did he contact you?" she asked.

"She didn't *contact* me, I met her in an open-air market in Kenya." I squirmed, trying to find a more comfortable position. It was difficult with my hands tied behind my back.

"What were you doing in Kenya?" she asked.

"That's where I was born and raised." I knew where this was going.

"But you live in America?"

"No, I live in Hong Kong," I said. "Well, I did until I came here."

"You're not American?"

"I am."

She looked confused. I didn't want to have to explain it to her.

"And who gave you permission to leave the planet?" she asked very seriously.

I laughed. "Are you kidding? Who was I supposed to consult—the Extra-Terrestrial Consulate?"

"You have a passport to travel outside the U.S., don't you?" she asked stubbornly.

I nodded. "Although I never really understood the point of them. They're supposed to grant you rights and protection outside your country or something. But it always felt more restricting to me—like governments do everything they can to discourage people from living abroad. And I think it's ridiculous."

"Well, if you want to live in another country, why don't you change citizenship?" She crossed her arms.

"Because you have to conform to a bunch of hogwash just to find yourself limited in new ways," I said. "People are more complicated than that—their heritages are more complicated than that."

"Right. And you obviously believe that people should be able to run all over the universe, doing whatever they want," she said acidly.

I knew she was being sarcastic, but it sounded pretty good to me. "You're telling me that if you met an alien on the street and she offered you transport to her world you would stop to ask permission?"

"Is that a serious question?" Her eyes conveyed her shock. "You could have just submitted yourself to alien slavery!"

"I know there's a lot of people in the world with evil intentions—but they are still the minority. And I've learned not to build relationships with new cultures on fear."

The Captain laughed cynically. "You're so naïve."

"Maybe. But I'm the one who's been living in an alien empire for three and a half years."

"Illegally."

"Are there *really* any laws against visiting aliens without federal permission? Whatever happened to America's enterprising spirit? You make it sound like one giant prison," I scoffed.

"And you've got some ego to think you are the best qualified person to enter negotiations with an alien species on behalf of Earth," she said.

"Why is the government so well equipped to represent Earth?" I asked. "I don't even feel like the federal government represents the majority of its citizens anymore. Your citizens aren't incompetent. And by the way, I'm hardly the first earthling to visit the Emirates."

The Captain's face paled.

"So how much trouble are you putting me in?" I asked soberly. My friends always said I was good at reading people, no matter what country I was in and this Captain didn't do things half-sies.

She pursed her lips and looked doubtful for the first time.

I tried to draw her out. "You could make an example of me. And I'd make a good scapegoat for all the problems of the next ten years." I knew my voice was hard and critical. I wanted her to think about her actions before she threw me to the bureaucratic lions. "I should have been born a hundred years ago," I muttered to myself.

"What took your parents to Kenya?"
"My father was a doctor."
"Humanitarian organization?"
"Yeah."
"In the city?"
I cleared my throat. "No, not really."

She looked at me studiously. I looked away—not because I was ashamed, but because of the onslaught of memories. They were always present like boulders balanced precariously on the edge of a slope, just waiting for a stone to tip off the avalanche. The avalanche had been tipped and the memories flooded in.

Thick red clay that caked the bottom of hard working feet, blaring traffic horns in the rain-soaked crevices of inner city Hong Kong, the way the rain swept across the savannah and filled my nostrils with the scent of wet grass, American malls decorated for Christmas and smelling like warm pretzels, the silhouette of the acacia trees in the blinding golden light of sunset, quiet hours where two hundred strangers all slept side by side on inter-continental flights, and the sounds and smells of market day. They were all a part of me. I looked back at her.

"I didn't grow up in your world," I said. "I grew up in some sort of spliced reality, patched into a single fabric by my impressionable mind. It existed while I believed in it. But I was its only citizen. And what's the good of being part of a blended nation no one else will recognize or even try to understand? They don't give blended passports."

The Captain cleared her throat several times. "They put me through six months of intensive training before they gave me this position. The man before me was invited to spend three days with the Shah in his palace. The second night he had a psychotic breakdown. They said it all ate away at him—the two moons, the smell of the air, the relentless singing, the tremors and the slight difference in gravity—not to mention the *kulli-kulli* bugs that are the size of your shoe."

"Yeah, they eat those," I said.

She rubbed her palms up and down her thighs. "My grandfather used to tell me that a flower that has plenty of water and sunshine will grow to be beautiful—until the weather changes. But the weeds which have to fight for existence, fight well in any weather."

I grimaced. "This has been a really weird day."

"I'm sorry, I'm not calling you a weed…" The Captain's eyebrows had relaxed considerably. Now they sat comfortably on her forehead, where they belonged. For a moment, I was reminded that I missed humans.

"I'm pretty sure you did," I teased.

She straightened her shoulders and her eyes dropped to my shoes. "Do you have somewhere to go?"

"What?"

"You were at the harvest ceremony thing, with the people picking up the leftovers." She was stuttering to find the right words.

"Gleaners. They were gleaners. I know it's not a common American term. Those harvesters and collectors were invented almost three hundred years ago, but the designs haven't been changed for the last seventy-five. There is an imperial ordinance that won't allow the collectors to surpass ninety-three percent efficiency—that way those in need can come and glean from what's left. Actually, some countries on Earth used to have a similar custom."

"So, you're struggling?"

I smiled. "I'm doing fine. I clearly don't have the bloodline to get any of the upper tier positions. And compared to the tradesmen, I'm completely incompetent. I tried an apprenticeship for about three months but in the end, I had to accept that compared to the average Emiratee craftsman I have significant physical limitations."

"So, you can't find work?"

"Well, the Emiratees aren't perfect. They have a complicated social structure—each tribe is steeped in its own tradition. They depend on each other for trade but they're too proud to learn each other's complex manner systems so they are constantly insulting each other. I'm good at picking up customs."

"You've become a middleman?"

"Yeah."

"They pay you for this?"

"They don't see it as a viable career. But they give me gifts to show their gratitude. I pick up the gleanings during the harvest season and barter for my other needs. I travel a lot, so I don't need much. It's a good system." I wondered where this conversation was heading. She showed a lot of interest for an officer dragging a fugitive home. "Well, it was fun while it lasted."

The Captain studied me for a long time. But I already knew what she would answer. Because her filters were up and her eyes were clear. Those keen eyes understood me.

"You're risking a lot out here on your own," she said quietly.

I smiled. I couldn't help it. "I was never going to live a safe life. This one suits me far better than a nine-to-five."

She untied my hands. "If anyone asks—we never ran into each other."

"Are you sure you're comfortable taking that kind of responsibility? I mean aren't there skyscrapers full of protocols against it?"

"Nothing that specifically addresses extra-terrestrial emigration." The transport was stopping. "I'm sorry. I'll have the transport take you back."

"Nah, the gleaning will be over." I waved a hand in dismissal.

"And it's my fault you missed it."

"There will be another gleaning tomorrow a hundred miles from here. I live flexibly."

The transport driver opened the door for us. I noticed the Captain flinch. She still wasn't accustomed to his striking features: his silver eyes matched his hair, contrasted by the dark brown-gray of his textured skin. I knew how she felt. At the beginning, it took some time for me to shake the feeling that they were all glaring at me.

"*Twate nxala xidobra. Nyenye.*" I spoke to the driver then turned back to the Captain. "He'll take you back to the Shah. I hope you enjoy the rest of your stay. Good luck, Captain."

"Good luck." The Captain returned stiffly to the transport. I noticed her two filters clamping firmly into place above her chocolate eyes. She would find out soon enough that pursing her lips like that was offensive to the Emiratee lower class. But she'd figure it out. Those eyebrows weren't about to have a panic attack. Maybe the Captain would be all right.

My attention was diverted as a swarm of Emiratee children assaulted me, their greedy fingers pinching my skin and pulling my hair.

"Hey, hey, hey! I'm not a pet," I chastised them in their own language. "Use the manners your parents taught you."

"Those only apply to other Emiratees," one cheeky little boy said.

"Oh, do I get to make up my own rules, too? Maybe I'll decide to string you up in a tree tonight. Go home to your parents for the evening meal."

The children scampered off, hooting and hollering like they were on a hunt. Their voices echoed like thunder because of the unique throat gland each Emiratee possesses. I was frequently teased for my weak voice, and on nights like tonight, when the sun was setting pink and blue, and the warmth hung in the air with the scent of earth, I envied them.

"Jeseeka."

I jumped at the Emiratee pronunciation of my name. One tiny little girl had remained behind.

"Will you take food with us?" She brushed a hand from the corner of her mouth, down her cheek and used all the words of a formal invitation. Her family had invited me, probably because they wanted something in return. Word traveled fast in these little Emiratee villages. I had not planned to be here tonight.

"No, no, little one. I will not burden you or your family." I gave the expected reply.

"Only your absence would be a burden, friend," she said solemnly.

I tried not to smile at her lisp. "I am not in the habit of burdening my friends," I answered, and we walked off together.

Having fulfilled her solemn responsibility, the little girl skipped beside me, a discordant tune escaping her lips with crystal clarity. The Emiratees adored music, although their standards of beautiful sounds were quite different than ours. It took me nearly eighteen months before I stopped shivering at the sound of it. Now it was as much a part of the landscape as the rocky hills, magenta-tinted fields, and twin moons. If the Emiratee song ever ceased to rise up from the land at all hours, the planet itself was likely to split open.

    The little girl led me up into the rocky hills, where all Emiratee villages were situated. They reserved the flat, fertile land for their crops. Their dwellings dotted the hillside like honeycombs—a mixture of mud, reeds, and long poles from the skinny *Tupi* trees that dotted the river basins. The little girl darted inside her family dwelling, but I waited outside for the family to greet me.

The mother came out with a fire-starting kit under her arm and knelt in front of me, touching a blessing to my feet. I reached into my pocket and dabbed a pungent substance to my eyes, the only way I had learned to produce tears on cue. I caught one from each eye with my left hand and placed the hand on her silvery mane: it was my blessing over her household.

    The formalities over with, she immediately began stoking the fire to prepare the meal. The Emiratees always cooked outside to help keep their houses cool. The evening meal was prepared just after sunset, the morning meal was prepared in the cool dark before dawn, and snacks were eaten throughout the day.

Now the father came to greet me. He took two of his own tears and placed them on my head. I knelt, touched my left hand to my lips, and touched his left knee. In the village five miles south, you were to use your right hand for these greetings, and in a village closer to the river, the women and men did not touch at all, but fulfilled the greetings with gestures that always ended no closer than one inch and no farther than three inches from the body. Emiratees from different villages were getting offended all the time. And this was just the greeting for inviting a guest to share a meal. They had ceremonies and formalities for all occasions. They were a people easily offended, but also easily pleased. My successful greeting tonight seemed to please them greatly. The formal mood was dropped and I was one of the family.

The little girl re-emerged from the dwelling with a series of gossamer threads, which I knew to be as fragile as they were thin. I guessed her to be the equivalent of four years old on Earth, but she began weaving those delicate threads into intricate patterns with the deftness of a seamstress. The fire was already blazing, and the mother began making the food preparations. I sat between the girl and her mother, across the fire from the father, who I suspected wanted to employ my services.

"Jeseeka," he began, "my cousin near the river wishes to give me a string of fish. But this week I am in the hills, hunting. If the fish go bad before I receive them, the stench will be on both our heads."

"I myself am heading to the northern gleaning," I replied matter-of-factly. My instincts told me that he had wronged his cousin somehow, and really wished to send a gift with me to make amends.

He waved his hand impatiently. "You need not think of gleaning when you are among family. Does not family take care of your needs?"

By which, of course, I knew he meant that he was willing to pay me. "I walk around so much, it is my way. I cannot accept all that my family would offer, just a sack full of *bula* roots. Please, do not give me more."

The father looked at the mother. She nodded.

"Perhaps your cousin would appreciate a gift for his great generosity," I continued.

The father looked pleased. "Yes, indeed. You speak well. I will send a gift to my cousin: three fine sheets of cloth, spun from the webs of the *kolli-kolli*."

I tried not to show my surprise. The value of that gift was probably half a year's wages. He must have really offended this cousin. But that wasn't my business. It was my job to make him feel at ease. Even now he was watching me nervously. "We often forget the value of family," I said. "He will understand the wisdom of this gift."

His eyes showed relief. "Yes, indeed. We must keep the bonds of family strong."

The matter was settled and my services had been purchased. There was always the slight chance that the situation was more complicated than it appeared to be. But I had talked my way out of hundreds of situations. I wasn't concerned. These Emiratee contracts were loose, anyway. Any party could back out up until the very last. If the cousin proved difficult, I would simply return with the cloth, and nothing more would be said about it.

Dark had fully settled across the land now and the fires of the other family units glowed like beacons in the mild night air. We ate a simple stew of roots and tubers with *kolli-kolli* meat and spices that reminded me of pepper and rosemary. I did not overstay my welcome, but promised to be back before light for the cloth. Then I slipped into the night to find a place to sleep.

Emiratee hospitality only extended so far. Their dwellings were very private places. Of course, if you mentioned anything about sleeping in the open, they would invite you in. But the cost of such a boarding arrangement was high, and it was one of the few things that made them truly uncomfortable. I had learned that it wasn't quite worth it, especially considering the favors they expected afterwards. The weather was always fine, except for two months of cold after harvest. But that was still a couple of weeks away, yet.

I climbed farther up the hills to where I had spotted two scrubby trees, pulled off my pack, and strung my hammock between them. Below me the fires of the village continued to dance, occasionally letting off a flurry of sparks into the warm night air. The voices of the Emiratees began to rise sporadically from around the village, weaving melodies and harmonies together as expertly as if they were standing side by side. Far away on the horizon, the twin moons began to rise. The first one, *Kelapoor*, was so large it must have been eight times the size of the moon on Earth. The second, *Muaomi*, was much smaller, but it glowed a distinct blue.

I closed my eyes in contentment, serenaded by the chilling voices of the Emiratees, bathed in the light of the alien moons, with a pocket knife under my pillow in case the burrowing rats got too friendly during the night. The night tremors began on cue, causing my hammock to sway back and forth gently, rocking me to sleep.

*****

I was startled awake, but not by the shrill calls of the lizards that rose just before dawn. The night sky had not completed its rotation. From the position of the twin moons, I guessed it was one in the morning. What had awoken me? Then I heard it again just as I saw the motion with my eye. A very nervous Emiratee was standing a few feet from my head, facing away from me, shuffling his feet back and forth, whistling very softly. I wondered which had made him more uncomfortable: the fact that he had to wake me from sleep, or the fact that I was sleeping outside. The Emiratees knew that I usually slept outside, but knowing and seeing were two completely different things in their culture. I slid out of my hammock with a grunt.

The Emiratee turned in relief. "It is fortunate that you happen to be awake, still idling here on the hillside before going to your dwelling for the night."

I raised an eyebrow in amusement, but he did not see it. "Yes," I stifled a yawn, "I was hoping a friend might come by to give me conversation." My mind was beginning to wake up. Why had he come here? Nothing like this had ever happened before.

He leapt on the excuse I had given him. "Yes! There are others this night who wish to make conversation, and they said to me, 'Go get the one from far away, whose skin changes color. We know she likes to make conversation late at night!' And so I am here."

Still a little grumpy from having been pulled from sleep, I frowned at his false representation of me. And just because my tan faded in the short winter, and my skin started each new planting season covered in a light sunburn, was no reason to characterize me as a chameleon. But a knot formed in my stomach. What was going on? Who would call for me in the middle of the night? Had the Captain changed her mind?

I began breaking camp in compliance and the Emiratee messenger sat down on a rock to wait for me.

But deep down inside I wondered if I shouldn't make a run for it. The more I thought about it, the more certain I was that the American Captain meant to arrest me. Maybe some of her superiors had arrived on the planet, or she had communicated with them. But as I had already told her, I had no intention of being criminalized for living on an alien planet. I could hide during the day and travel up north until this whole thing blew over. Maybe in the meantime she'd stumble upon another unsuspecting earthling to blame.

But guilt tugged at my stomach. To abandon this messenger and force him to return empty handed would be shameful. Word would spread quickly and my reputation as a middle man might be tarnished. It wasn't fair for the Captain to send him after me. She should have come herself. My gut instincts had served me well my whole life. I wasn't about to put this Emiratee, or any others for that matter, in the middle of an Earth dispute. They didn't deserve that. So, as stupid as it may have been, I followed him down the hill, through the village, to the waiting transport.

The ride wasn't incredibly long, but I spent it deep in thought, mentally exploring all my options. Perhaps my cooperation would be worth something. Even if they arrested me and hauled me back to Earth, I would get one phone call, right? I could call my sister-in-law and she could get in touch with the media. Or a lawyer. Or maybe both. Would they throw me in prison? Or just penalize me somehow? Okay, so maybe

I wouldn't actually tell the media, but I could threaten to. But they'd probably just give me a gag order. I was no good at this planning ahead thing. I needed to see how things actually stood—what they were going to do to me. Then I'd find a loophole. There was always a loophole.

The transport pulled to a stop in front of the Shah's palace, confirming my suspicions. It was a great building, carved directly into a small mountain of red rock, which must've helped keep it cool inside, even during the hottest time of the year. I was promptly escorted inside without explanation.

The floor was paved with cool river rocks of various shades of green. Great red columns supported the arched ceiling where rows of artificial fronds swayed endlessly back and forth, to circulate the air. Nobles stood in clusters, whispering. It was easy to distinguish them by the draping robes of translucent cloth, woven from the webs of the *kolli-kolli*. The material caught any light around it and refracted it into ruby red shades. I had never seen so much of it in one place. A night tremor shook the ground but evoked no response from anyone in the palace.

My guide led me down a hallway and into a fine room where I immediately realized my assessment of the situation had been false. The Captain sat huddled in a corner, holding her head and muttering to herself while rocking back and forth. I groaned internally.

"How long has she been like this?" I asked.

"A servant found her three hours ago, because she was making noise."

"But how was she at the evening meal?" I asked. "Please find me someone who was there, and get some water."

I knelt in front of the Captain, suddenly realizing that I didn't even know her name. "Hey there, Captain. Remember me? I'm the girl you tackled at the gleaning today."

She shook her head as if trying to get rid of my voice. I struggled to hear what she was mumbling to herself.

"225 Rutherford Way, Escalon, California," she whispered.

I sat down in front of her and crossed my legs. "Escalon, huh? I've never been. But I had a great uncle who grew walnuts in Modesto."

She kept rocking, but her mumbling grew less distinct and I knew she was listening.

"My dad said he used to swim in the irrigation canals when he was a kid. But I've seen that water, it's nasty. I guess you'd do anything to keep cool as a kid during summer in the San Joaquin valley." I was trying to add in as many familiar references as possible. "It gets blazing hot. But you can get the best fruits and nuts there—straight from those little stands on the sides of the road."

The Captain opened her mouth to speak. Her lips fumbled for a moment. "Irrigation canals aren't safe," she stammered. Fresh tears slid down her cheeks.

"It's okay," I said. "You're gonna be okay."

"Am I going to wake up?" She cried. "Or was it all a dream? Was my family a dream?"

"No sweetheart." She was probably ten years older than me, but she looked so young and fragile. "*This* is the dream. You're gonna wake up and tell everyone about this crazy dream."

My Emiratee helper had returned with a glass of water.

"Look at this guy," I said with a smirk as I pulled a small packet of crushed herbs from my pack and sprinkled it into the water. "Isn't he crazy? You must've eaten a half-cooked hamburger or something. Didn't your mom ever teach you not to eat fast food?"

She was sipping on her water now between sobs. Her eyes were red and her hands trembled. Another night tremor shook the ground beneath us. She leaned back into the walls. "Not again, not again," she mumbled.

And then an oblivious Emiratee struck up a piercing tune outside and she clutched her ears and began muttering her address again, over and over. I placed a comforting hand on her leg until the herbs in her drink took effect and she passed out.

"You convinced her to go to sleep," my Emiratee companion said.

"Yeah, I convinced her," I said. These herbs had no effect on them. "Did you find someone who was at the evening meal with her?"

A second Emiratee stepped forward. "She seemed very uncomfortable at evening meal, which made us all uncomfortable."

"Uncomfortable, how?" I asked patiently, knowing that the word uncomfortable encompassed a whole spectrum of behavior.

"She started to become incredibly bored, staring at her plate. We thought maybe she didn't approve of the food, so we brought her some roasted desert spider and *pakwik*. And she smiled and nodded, but she didn't eat it. And then her eyes were sleepy and red and she began to twitch when we spoke to her. We thought she must be angry. So, we all left the room graciously and she returned to her quarters. The Shah said we must sing her the chorus of repentance between friends or she would give a bad report to her people."

I sighed, understanding how several things had been misunderstood at the evening meal. That chorus of repentance was enough to do any human in. Two years ago, it might have sent me into a nervous breakdown.

"Help me get her on the bed," I said.

Both Emiratees backed up, shaking their heads. It was bad enough that they were in her room right now. I sighed and pulled the Captain towards me, hoisting her tall, muscular form over my shoulder with a loud grunt, then stumbled over to the bed and laid her out.

The Emiratees were backing up slowly towards the door. "Then she will be able to continue her stay in the morning?"

"No," I said bluntly, "I don't believe she can continue her stay in the morning."

"But she will give a good report of us to her people?"

I frowned. "I don't know."

"The Shah requests your presence," they said, then darted out the door, leaving me alarmed.

The Shah? I did not know the customs for greeting royalty. I had never had to learn them. I could make an educated guess, but what if I was wrong and I offended him? I shut the door tightly behind me and followed my companions through the halls of the palace, trying to decide on my greeting.

We came out in a grand hall, simple in its construction and decoration, as the rest of the palace was. In the center was a raised dais where the Shah sat on his throne. At the foot of the dais was a bubbling fountain, dancing in lights of blue and green. Above it all, two large mechanized panels had been opened to reveal the glittering stars and let the night air waft in.

I had only ever seen the Shah three times and only at a distance. He was a pudgy old man with a mouth that perpetually turned down and unusually large eyes. I approached the dais at the pace of my two companions. They stopped and knelt at the bottom of the stairs, but I proceeded halfway up before kneeling. I dabbed my eyes liberally with my tear-inducing mixture, waited until my fingers were shining with tears, then extended them palms up toward him, with my head lowered between them. A moment later I felt his fingers grasp mine and pull slightly upwards. I raised my head. He took one hand and pressed my tears to his lips. His mouth was still sagging at the corners, but his large eyes were pleased. I knew whether or not it had been customary, that my greeting was well accepted.

The Shah resumed his seat on his throne and gestured to the floor on his right. I seated myself there and crossed my legs, blinking rapidly to try to dispel the collected water in my eyes. I had learned to produce tears on cue like the Emiratees, but I had yet to learn how to make my eyes dry instantly afterwards, like theirs did.

He studied me with a curious expression on his face, and then he spoke. "No other human has attempted to produce the tears of greeting," he said. "Who are you?"

"Your people call me Jeseeka, good father," I replied with lowered eyes.

"But where do you come from? There seems to be some knowledge of you in several of my villages. But I was not aware that your people had sent a second envoy."

"I am not an envoy," I said. "I came here three years ago with one of your tradesman."

"And yet you are not ill like the Kapten?" He asked in shock.

"No, good father."

"Jeseeka, may I hold counsel with you as with a friend?" He asked softly.

I held my breath. I knew he was permitting me to converse with him as if he were my equal, and it terrified me. The social ranks and customs were so important to the Emiratees. But I lifted my eyes in compliance. How could I refuse him? His eyes, rich, silvery, and utterly penetrating, were waiting for mine.

"I am afraid of what will happen when the Kapten goes home," he confided. "I am afraid that her people will not understand it."

"Is it true that she is the second to return in this state?" I asked timidly.

"It is true."

"They will not understand it, and they tend to fear what they do not understand."

"Will it plant aggression in their hearts?" he asked.

"Maybe. Unless they are made somehow to understand."

"If I cut our world off from them, I fear this will fester in their hearts until they have discovered a way to come here on their own. But if I request another envoy to come understand, will he not become ill like the others?"

"It is a difficult position," I said. "Perhaps you regret extending the hand of friendship so soon, when clearly my people were not ready."

"And yet are you not here, holding counsel with me?"

"I am not—" I hesitated, suddenly overcome with unexpected emotion. "I am nobody in my world. I have no trade, no village. I am like an outcast; I do not fit anywhere. And so I have come to your world to be an outcast among strangers. Do you understand?"

"These new tears I see are of emotion, are they not, human?" He asked.

I nodded.

"You know much about us, but still you do not know our ways. My servants saw you at the gleaning today. But do you know the purpose behind it?"

"So that no one goes hungry."

"That is the result. The purpose is to remind ourselves that inefficiency can be as useful to some as efficiency is to others. Everything has a purpose in this world. If it has no purpose to me, it has purpose to someone or something else. You say that you are an outcast in your world, with no purpose or value. And yet you have fallen on us in our time of need, perhaps to prevent conflict between our two worlds. Do you think that perhaps this could be your purpose?"

His words seared my heart like a hot iron and I couldn't have stopped the tears even if I had wanted to. He gave me a cloth to wipe my eyes.

"If you are to go, you must leave in the morning with the Kapten. Consider my words well."

I was escorted to a simple room and I entered it without protest. But after a few minutes I slipped out the window, searching for somewhere to hang my hammock. I was not going to spend tonight of all nights, indoors. I eventually found a crevice of perfect width in the rock mountain behind the palace. I anchored the two ends of the hammock into the crevice walls, then slipped into the closest thing I had had to a home over the past three and a half years.

The sun would be up in a few hours. It probably wasn't even worth sleeping. But if I was going to return to Earth tomorrow, there was no better way to spend my last hours than gazing at the night sky of this world. The twin moons were already approaching the far horizon, but I could still see them from my vantage point in the mouth of the crevice. The phosphorescent blue glow of *Muaomi* was always comforting to me. I tried to remember what the moon looked like back on Earth and in my memory it seemed so very small. A night tremor swayed my hammock while a soft breeze stirred, smelling of rich clay and warm cut grass.

My father had always believed that each one of us had a unique purpose in life. Was this mine? It seemed preposterous to think that of all the people on

Earth, I was the one meant to act as ambassador between Earth and this remarkable world. Another night tremor swayed my hammock, this one stronger in force, and somewhere a couple hundred meters to my left an Emiratee took up a night song in tones that sent shivers down my spine. Could I teach the people of Earth to understand this place? To grow to love it as I had? Were they ready? In the back of my mind I heard the voice of my father from long ago. "You won't know until you try."

GOVERNMENT MAN

The Light Behind Shadows Part 1

THE CONTACT

Caleb Weiss stumbled through the sea of spectators, his dingy denim coat and moldy beanie a stark contrast to the standard issue, gray wool pea coats surrounding him. Men and women parted for him well in advance, reluctant to get too close to him. But he kept up a drunken shuffle to make sure their eyes avoided him and returned back to the speaker on the podium. He needed to be invisible.

A rich, gravelly voice was talking to the assembled crowd. "The defense of this nation is not always a glamorous job. But it is necessary, as we saw ten years ago. As we have re-expanded our military for the first time in fifty years, a couple of things have become apparent, including the incredible toll on the families of our men and women in service and undercover."

Caleb may have looked inebriated, but his senses were finely tuned. He was listening to the speaker on the platform, keenly aware of the reactions of the crowd, but his eyes were searching for a very particular statue. There it was. He didn't approach it head on, but meandered a little through the crowd before advancing on the statue. He leaned up against it, as if to steady himself, until his eyes caught sight of the white piece of paper wedged in between the statue and the pedestal. The grimy piece of paper had six words on it: "I'm in the crapper. Turn around." Caleb turned, spotted the men's restroom across the plaza, and began making his way through the crowd. Enthusiastic applause sounded all around him and then the speaker continued.

"You, dear people, voted for me because I vowed to take care of our servicemen and their families. And I am so thankful to live in a society that prioritizes the well-being of the men and women who serve and defend it. Brothers and sisters, in the last eight years we have seen a seventy-five percent decrease in depression, anxiety, and other mental illness among the families of our servicemen. And I think it goes without saying that the longevity of our servicemen increases when their families are content and supportive."

Another round of applause broke out. And Caleb had arrived at his destination. He glanced around briefly before pulling open the door to the restroom and slipping through. As the door closed behind him, it muffled the sound of the public address system. But he had heard the propaganda before. His attention was entirely focused on the man in front of him.

He sat slumped against the wall, an olive green beanie only partially covering his long, silver hair. He was hemmed in by a tattered backpack and a brown paper bag with a bottle in it and he reeked of alcohol, cigarettes, and body odor.

The older man looked Caleb up and down. "Do I know you?"

Caleb tossed the man a brown bag, similar to the one on his left side.

He examined the contents with a grin, "Oh, I think I remember you, now. You're that pesky G-man who's always looking for information."

"I wouldn't complain too loudly if I was you. I'm keeping your sorry carcass out of prison and I meet your prices."

"Yeah, but you attract trouble faster than a clean car attracts mud." The man sighed. "One of these days I might just decide that the clanger offers me a little more peace of mind. What is it you want from me today?"

"I need the time and place of their next meeting," Caleb said.

The man groaned and closed his eyes, then held out his paper bag, pleadingly. "Take it back, I don't want it."

"Cut the theatrics, Bradshaw."

"Nah, really, man. It's not worth it. Even I got my limits. If you get outed as a government man and anyone finds out I told you, I'm dead."

Caleb scrutinized the man for a moment, then suddenly grabbed his collar and dragged him to his feet, nearly choking him against the wall, "If you're more afraid of these terrorists than your own government, I can change that. I can leave a tip for the League that you've been narking to the government. How long do you think you'll last? Huh? Now if you cooperate with me, there's the chance that they won't find out."

"Get your hands off of me, you filthy scum. You pretend you're so much better than the League, but your government is just another brand of terrorists. They don't have a moral conscience. They just want to keep us all under control."

"Yeah, yeah. Save your conspiracy talk for later. What's it gonna be?"

"Alright, alright," Bradshaw surrendered. "Back off, bulldog."

Caleb let go of Bradshaw, who slumped against the wall in a coughing fit.

"Well?" Caleb asked unsympathetically.

"I need time," Bradshaw gasped. "The next meeting isn't until next month. They don't give out the location in advance."

Caleb squatted down in front of him and smoothed the man's jacket from where it had been ruffled.

Bradshaw cringed.

"If you're lying to me…"

"Have I ever lied to you, Weiss?"

"No. And if you know what's good for you, you'll keep it that way," Caleb threatened. "Do I look like a man who's bluffing?"

"Nah. You look like a man with the power of an evil government behind him."

Caleb rolled his eyes and stood to his feet. "You'll contact me as soon as you know anything?"

"Yeah, man. I already said I would."

"If I don't hear from you within the month, I will find you. And you'll wish you'd never been born, do you understand?"

"Geez, you know our country's going downhill when its honored veterans and government agents are nothing but a bunch of thugs."

"I'm glad we understand each other. Take care of yourself, Bradshaw." Caleb left the bathroom without looking back. He yanked his beanie and jacket off, despite the frosty weather, and dumped them in the nearest trashcan hoping he could discard Bradshaw's words as easily. He hated this part of his job. If his wife ever really saw what he did, she'd be horrified. Sometimes he was horrified himself. But he had taken an oath. Someone had to do the dirty work, right? And if it saved lives and kept the general population safe, then maybe he could live with it. Besides, it wasn't forever. If he hung in there and paid his dues, he could get out as soon as his contract was up.

No one in the crowd paid him any heed this time. Their attention was riveted on the podium, where the speaker was still talking. He had moved on from veteran affairs to food regulations. Caleb wondered ruefully if the audience knew their food rations were laced with mood-altering drugs, whether they would be clapping so enthusiastically. True, it didn't affect everyone. But it affected enough people for the government to consider it worth the effort. And they were stingy with their money. Caleb made his way back to headquarters. He had reports to fill out and then an interrogation to help with. He wasn't looking forward to it. Captain Rush was in charge of it, and Rush always took it further than Caleb was comfortable with. But tomorrow…tomorrow would be a better day.

TOMORROW

The morning was blue. Not in any profound emotional sense—Sarah had barely been awake long enough to have doleful thoughts about the day. It was blue the way the mountains look blue from far away. Perhaps some of that mysterious morning air found on mountaintops had migrated to ensconce the city streets. Sarah did not stop to admire it, but she breathed it in with the voracity of first life.

Her destination was a small, local-run coffee shop and the caffeine and solace it provided. A network of soggy, half-frozen puddles barricaded the door, testing her dedication and ingenuity. She growled at the inconvenience, blaming the world for this most recent attack on her peace of mind. But safe inside the door the small battle was already forgotten and a smile slipped back on her face.

"Your usual today, Sarah?" the barista greeted her.

"Make it a triple, Gino."

"Long week?"

"You have no idea," she confirmed while fishing in her purse for her wallet, "I've been vomited on three times. And I don't know what it is, but all my parents have been on edge."

"It's the winter."

"It's been winter for eight weeks now."

"Exactly. Christmas vacation is over, but winter is still here. Everybody's getting cabin fever," Gino said knowingly.

"Well, I guess I'm their favorite punching bag right now," she sighed.

"Don't let it get to you. They're lucky to have you."

"I know. I guess I'm just tired. I haven't been sleeping well."

"How're the folks?" he asked.

"I mentioned to my mom that I'm thinking about moving out and she went completely pale. Mom, I'm twenty-six not sixteen. I mean I'm grateful they let me live with them through school but it's like I got stuck in this rut and I don't understand it. I want to move forward."

"That's how it is with the baby," Gino replied confidently, "We won't let Joseph move out until after we're dead, eh Joey?" he playfully ruffled the hair of the ten-year-old boy sitting on a stool to his left.

Sarah smiled. "Joey, don't let him bully you," she responded good-naturedly, "You call me if you need an advocate."

Gino handed over her coffee.

"Thank you."

"Have a good weekend, Sarah."

"If I can survive today, I will." She had dragged herself out of bed early in order to guarantee some time with her coffee before work, so she made her way to a quiet little corner.

The bell above the door vibrated ferociously, heralding the entrance of another customer. Sarah's eyes gravitated toward the movement out of habit, but the face she saw was not one she had been expecting. It took her a moment to recognize him. He paused in the doorway, his eyes fastened purposefully on her face. She felt her ivory skin turn ghostly white before being brushed with a telltale stroke of red. Her eyes dropped to the table in front of her. This must have been why she had been so tense all week. But how could she have known he would be here?

Her ears were trained to pick up the whispered conversations of inattentive students. Now they heard him ordering coffee. She could walk out right now. There was still time. But there were things she wanted to say to him. And when would she see him again? The echo of his footsteps marked his progress across the floor. She did not look at him when he stood beside her. Not even when he pulled out the chair to her left.

"That seat's taken," she couldn't help herself. She knew it was childish. But didn't he deserve it? He decided to take the high road and moved around the table. His quiet grace irked her. "So is that one."

Hesitation.

"I'll move as soon as it's wanted," Caleb promised gently.

She knew she had lost the first scrimmage.

"It's good to see you," the depth of emotion in his voice pierced her heart like a harpoon. But she was not prepared to throw her white flag just yet.

"I wouldn't really know, would I?" she answered coldly.

He accepted her anger like it was his duty. "Are you going to be angry at me every time I see you?"

She looked at him for the first time, "Does it make me angry when I remember what happened? Yes."

"Sarah, I did it for your own good."

"You had no right to make that decision for me," she said hotly, pulling out her lesson plans.

"We both know if I hadn't you wouldn't be able to move forward with your life."

"The way I'm so obviously moving forward now? I canceled my last two dental appointments, do you know why? I knew that perky little assistant would ask me about my love life. And do you know what I'd have to tell her? 'No, I'm not dating. I'm not in love. I'm twenty-six and I never really have been.'"

"You know that's not true," he whispered.

"No, I don't, Caleb. You decided that I shouldn't ever know whether that's true or not."

He looked at her with compassion, but not regret. "How are your parents?"

She hesitated, "Protective."

"And your students?"

"Adorable," she said begrudgingly, "Even when they're puking on me they're still adorable. Although I keep chewing out Valero for transferring me from inner city, and I should probably stop that."

"Yeah, you probably should."

"Working with privileged parents is twice as hard."

"It's not permanent," he said.

"It feels permanent. I've been looking at my budget—trying to save up to buy a house or go back to school, or something."

"Your parents won't let you make any poor financial decisions."

"I get short with them a lot," she admitted.

"They understand."

She was still scribbling away on her papers, avoiding his eyes. He watched her contentedly, as if none of his life had made any sense until this moment. And she pretended to ignore him, aware of similar feelings but wanting to punish him a little bit longer.

Gino had turned on an album with soft vocals to ease his sleepy customers into their day. But the sky outside did not share his consideration. Half-frozen drops of rain began pelting the asphalt, pinging off the tops of worn-down cars, and tapping persistently on the windows like a petulant child. Not to be outdone, the wind awoke with a temper, howling its grievances to anyone who would listen.

Sarah's uninvited companion rose abruptly, retreating toward the door with the same singular purpose that had brought him in. She watched his back in alarm, her busy pen suddenly idle, her large brown eyes suddenly unguarded. Would he just leave like that? Without another word? Hadn't he seen through it all—that it was just a tough charade? Did he really believe that she didn't want him here?

She shoved back her chair with violent force, not even registering its wooden scream against the cold floor. But he heard it and his hand hesitated on the door as he turned back.

"Are you leaving?" She had never mastered the art of subtlety. Her desperation rang through each word clearly as her arms hung limply by her side.

Caleb couldn't help smiling. "I'm going to my car...to get my computer, because you seem determined to ignore me."

"But if you leave the room..."

"You can watch me through the window," he pointed to his car.

She didn't sit down. The tears threatened to come and when he saw them he changed his course. She met him halfway, throwing her arms around his neck and painting his face with tears and kisses.

"I'm sorry I'm such a brat."

"You don't have to apologize."

"I have to be mad at you, at least at first. But I want you here."

"I know, I know." He stroked her hair as she cried into his shoulder for a few minutes. No one in the sleepy coffee shop disturbed them, but the frozen rain and icy wind made renewed charges at the window pane, as if trying desperately to drive the couple apart. The walls stood, at least for now.

"How long are you here?" Sarah asked.

"Thirty-six hours leave," he answered.

She sighed angrily at him.

"But I've been promised a whole week in the near future," he added.

"How near?"

"Maybe in about three weeks."

"So after I'm dead, basically?"

"You can't die. It's in my contract. You are the safest citizen in this country. I've made sure of it," he tucked a stray piece of hair behind her ear.

"The unhappiest citizen in this country. The worst part? Half the time I don't even know why I'm unhappy. I look around and everything seems to be going well in my life except for the little part of me that remembers you in my dreams."

"I'm sorry, Sarah. You know that I am. The Agency won't undo it until my assignment is finished."

"So tomorrow when you leave, I'll forget again?" She asked as she always did.

"Yes," Caleb answered.

"And I'll be alone again?"

"Just for a few months."

"Do you have my ring?" she asked.

He pulled at a chain around his neck, producing a set of dog tags with two rings attached. She watched anxiously as he fished it off the chain and slid it on her left hand. And then she breathed freely as she hadn't done in months.

ABOUT THREE WEEKS LATER

Mr. and Mrs. Johnson were not rebellious folk. They watched all the highest grossing films and bought the store brands that used cute animals in their commercials. They didn't balk at the standard issue clothes used to differentiate the middle class from those less fortunate. They attended every social event they were invited to, even that quilting party that neighbor Agnes hosted to save endangered species no one had ever heard of before. Mrs. Johnson suspected that neighbor Agnes was secretly trying to fund her expensive taste in jewelry, and Mrs. Johnson told her husband so. But she attended all the same.

Mr. Johnson went golfing every Tuesday with the other men on floor fifty-seven, he always ordered the Cobb salad at lunch, and he always kept the conversation on harmless topics, like the weather. But both Mr. and Mrs. Johnson were concerned about their daughter, Sarah. They were so concerned that they even began to talk about behind closed doors.

"It ain't right," Mr. Johnson said one night before bed.

"Will you keep your voice down?" Mrs. Johnson hissed at him. "You know neighbor Agnes holds a cup to the wall!"

"I'm sure she does no such thing."

"I caught her doing it!" his wife insisted. "Only she was eavesdropping on the Smiths on the other side. Sometimes I wonder if she isn't a government spy."

"The government has much more capable people to use as spies," Mr. Johnson replied.

Mrs. Johnson lowered her eyes at the reminder and began furiously pulling back the bed covers and plumping the pillows.

"Which brings me back to what I was saying before I was so rudely interrupted." He paused as if waiting for her to protest. But her eyes remained downcast. "I don't know how much longer Sarah can take it," he finished.

"Well she doesn't have a choice, does she?" Mrs. Johnson snapped. "Why couldn't she have fallen in love with that nice banker from your office Christmas party?"

"Well, she didn't. She fell in love with Caleb. And he was the best thing that happened to her."

"Until he decided to sign his life over," Mrs. Johnson muttered bitterly.

"The young man wanted to serve his country. I understand that. I don't think any of us could have known what it cost."

"If she comes to me one more time with a proposal for how to move her life forward...I don't know what I'll do," Mrs. Johnson's voice was beginning to break. She sat on the side of the bed, clasping her hands to keep them from trembling.

Mr. Johnson came and put his arm around her consolingly.

"It won't last forever," he assured her. "Caleb's contract will be up and the Agency will return all of Sarah's memories. And she'll be able to start building a life with the husband she loves."

"Do we know that?" Mrs. Johnson asked. "What if they keep finding reasons to extend his contract? I heard they did that to Patricia's son." She put a hand to her mouth to stifle a sob. "Sarah's mind may not remember her husband when he's gone, but her heart does. And I'm afraid it's breaking..."

Mr. Johnson held his wife close as she cried. But he had no words to comfort her. The same fears had been lurking in his own mind over the last year. Whispers and rumors had begun circulating in his office—stories of broken promises and shady dealings. When had the people started to become afraid of their own government?

The doorbell rang suddenly, making them both start. Mr. Johnson frowned, glancing at the clock. Who would be visiting at 11:00 at night.

"Wash your face, dear," he said gently, pulling on his robe and donning his slippers. He padded down the carpeted hallway of their condo, passing Sarah's room. The light was out. She could sleep through anything. His hand trembled as he opened the front door.

A man in a black coat and hat flashed a government insignia at him. "Sorry to disturb you, Mr. Johnson," his voice was insincere, "But I'm going to need a few minutes of your time."

"Of course," Mr. Johnson nodded and held the door open, "Anything for a servant of the government."

The man stalked in arrogantly and surveyed the living room with disdain. "Is your wife at home?"

"Yes, of course. I'll have her put on her robe. Would you like some tea?"

"No, thank you."

Mr. Johnson nodded again and then slipped down the hallway to retrieve his wife. When they returned to the living room they found their guest sitting on the edge of one of the armchairs, his fingers steepled in front of him, and a look of impatience on his face.

"Mrs. Johnson, I presume?"

"Yes," Mrs. Johnson put a hand to the curlers in her hair, "Forgive me, we weren't expecting company."

Their guest gestured to the opposite couch authoritatively and waited for them to comply. They sat down timidly, clasping hands instinctually.

"Is this about Caleb?" Mrs. Johnson ventured boldly.

"Hush, dear," Mr. Johnson squeezed her hand. "He'll tell us."

"Your son-in-law has been killed in service to his country," the man recited emotionlessly.

Mrs. Johnson gasped.

"I'm here to ensure his family is taken care of, and the reputation of his government remains intact. I understand you are the guardians of his wife during his contracted service?"

"Yes. Our daughter, Sarah."

"Does she live with you?"

"She's just asleep," Mrs. Johnson gestured in the direction of Sarah's bedroom.

The government man's eyes followed the motion keenly.

"Shall I wake her?"

"She won't know who we're talking about," Mr. Johnson reminded his wife sadly.

"Because she's taken the memory treatment?" the government man asked.

"Yes, sir." Mr. Johnson answered quietly.

"Good. That's all I need to know," the man stood to his feet and pulled out what appeared to be his car keys.

Mr. and Mrs. Johnson exchanged a confused glance.

"Will she never remember him?" Mr. Johnson's voice was full of heartache.

"No," the government man replied drily, fumbling with his key chain. "Coincidentally, neither will you." He held up a small device and activated it. A fine mist exploded into the air and was almost immediately inhaled by Mr. and Mrs. Johnson. The nearly invisible nanites did their work in a matter of seconds, attacking every memory associated with Caleb Weiss. The government man was in and out of Sarah's room in seconds and out the door before Mr. and Mrs. Johnson could figure out what they were doing on the couch at 11:00pm on a week day.

NOT DEAD

Caleb Weiss lay in a puddle of his own blood. His tongue felt thick, his limbs heavy, and a throbbing pain in his left shoulder warned him that if he moved, he would regret it. But his first cohesive thought was of Sarah. It didn't matter what state he was in; he'd rise from the dead to get back to Sarah. He had promised her that he would always come back.

He moved his head to see how bad the damage was and fiery pain shot down his spine. For a moment he thought every bone in his body was cracked. It didn't matter. He'd crawl his way to his wife, even if it took five years. He'd just rather there be an easier option. He took a quick breath and then rolled himself over, ignoring the excruciating pain and trying to remember what had happened.

Bradshaw had finally contacted him, giving him a time and a place. Then that dirty rat had shown up stone drunk and outed him. Weiss wouldn't have made it out alive if that sewage drain hadn't been nearby. That must be why he felt like a water-logged piece of raw meat, and why he smelled like one, too. But he was alive. And he had names and faces now. Maybe he could use it as leverage to get out of his contract sooner. Maybe, just maybe, he and Sarah could finally be together again. First he had to get himself somewhere safe.

It took him nearly ten minutes just to get on his hands and knees. That throbbing ache in his shoulder was a gunshot wound. His ribs were cracked, wrist broken, and he likely had a concussion. But he was alive and he had Sarah. That was all that mattered.

The sewage drain must have carried him miles from the city. The city was nowhere in sight. He was surrounded by barren wasteland as far as the eye could see. It might be eaten up in fifteen years as the city expanded, but for now it was just useless rock and sand.

Caleb walked all day and still couldn't catch sight of the skyline. Granted, his pace was anything but rapid. When night fell he did his best to bury himself in the sand and hoped desperately for sleep. But sleep didn't come. His constant shivering exacerbated his injuries and kept his pain level high. Sometime in the early morning he thought he saw Sarah's face. But was that a dream or a hallucination? He rose with first light and forced his stiff limbs into motion. The terrain was growing a little more familiar. But it still took nearly eight hours before he reached the outskirts of the city.

Mothers glanced at him nervously and pulled their children close. He didn't blame them. He must look like a walking nightmare. It was another mile before he found a gas station with a payphone. He picked up the receiver and punched in his code.

They came and picked him up right away, almost as if they were in a hurry. He was rushed into headquarters, run through multiple scans and then placed in an accelerated healing chamber. They must have drugged him, too, because he woke up completely refreshed. But he knew he hadn't passed out on his own. He wouldn't have let himself pass out, if it meant one more hour without seeing his wife.

The chamber's lid popped open above him and he pulled himself out, noticing the significant decrease in pain. It wasn't completely gone, but compared to the state he had been in, he was a new man, now.

"Sergeant Weiss," a corporal greeted him. "It's good to see you up and about, sir. Captain Rush's ready to debrief you."

Caleb nodded at the man and then made his way to conference room one. He knew the way well enough. The captain sat at the table with an open file in front of him. He did not stand when Caleb entered the room and saluted, but gestured to the seat across from him with his pen.

"How are you feeling, sergeant?"

"Much better, sir."

"Good, good."

"If I may ask, sir…how long was I in there?"

"Ten days."

Caleb blanched. What must the Johnsons think? Maybe it was a blessing that at least Sarah wouldn't be worrying. He had had his doubts about the memory treatment protocol. But maybe the government knew what it was doing after all. At least this once, his wife had been spared pain.

"What do you remember from your last mission, sergeant? Did you actually meet the League?"

"Pardon me, sir, but how long is this debrief going to take?"

Captain Rush squinted his eyes at him.

"I'd just really like to contact my in-laws and tell them I'm alright. It won't take long."

"That won't be necessary."

"Do you mean you've already been in contact with them?"

"Son, the League sent us your dog tags, and took credit for your death. We didn't hear from you for twenty-four hours. We called it."

Caleb stared at his superior office blankly.

"We pronounced you dead and followed protocol. The Johnsons were informed of your death and then given a permanent wipe."

Caleb blinked.

"Grief is a funny thing. It can motivate the most reasonable citizens to say things about their government that they'd regret."

Caleb blinked again. "The Johnsons have no memory of me?"

"It's better this way. They were a sentimental couple—a little too prone to dangerous emotions, like bitterness and misplaced resentment."

"Then let me see my wife. Please. I know you want to hear about what happened, but I've just been to the grave and back. I'll think more clearly after I see my wife."

"Sergeant Weiss, I don't think you understood me. All of the Johnsons were wiped. Your wife's temporary treatment was supplemented with a long-term solution. Some of those temporary treatments have slipped in the past."

Caleb's vision began to black out. "Are you telling me that my wife won't ever remember who I am?"

"You are ordered, under Legislation XVII, Article 5.5 to give up your privilege to ever see your wife again. This government is not prepared to risk any sort of malfunction causing a public scandal. Do you understand me, sergeant?"

"No, I'm not sure that I do."

"Then let me make it abundantly clear to you. You have fallen into an unfortunate situation, my friend. Most of our servicemen don't find out about the permanent wipe protocol. It happens after they're dead and does no harm to anyone. But here we are. Your government has acted on your behalf and now your duty is to ensure your government does not lose the respect of its people. You will never mention your wife again or attempt to see her. Are we clear on the terms?"

Caleb began nodding his head and didn't seem to be able to stop.

Captain Rush frowned. But his day was about to get a whole lot worse.

Caleb flipped the table in one fluid motion, leaped over its upturned side and knocked the captain unconscious with a single blow. He grabbed the man's ID badge and stuffed his sidearm into his belt, concealing it under his t-shirt. He took a deep breath in an attempt to steady his trembling hands. Then he exited the conference room with as much confidence as he could muster.

"Hey, Weiss!" a man called out, "Is your meeting with Captain Rush over? I need his signature."

"What? Um, I don't know."

"What do you mean, you don't know? Weren't you just talking to him?" The man had his handle on the door.

Caleb kept walking, but his mouth had gone completely dry. He heard the door creak open and an expletive slip out of the man's mouth.

"Guards, stop that man, he assaulted a superior officer!"

Caleb broke into a run. The daylight streaming through the glass door ahead tempted him like a mirage. It was only fifty feet away. But those fifty feet could spell his death. A guard came at him from his right. He ducked and jammed a knee into the man's groin, then hurled him into the guard approaching from his left. Caleb didn't even feel his partially-healed injuries anymore. He might as well have been invincible.

He managed to run ten feet before another guard assaulted him from behind, attempting to put him in a stranglehold. Caleb side-stepped and swept the man's legs out from beneath him, sending him crashing to the floor. They would start using weapons, soon. Tasers if he was lucky, projectiles if they were desperate. But it was too late to stop him. He had smelled the fresh air and his sheer determination would drive him through that open door, whether he was riddled with bullets or not.

Fortunately, a guard with a shield came at him next. Caleb saw him out of the corner of his eyes, stopped suddenly, bent his knees, and shoved upward with his shoulder against the shield as hard as he could. It hit the unsuspecting guard just below the nose, and a torrent of blood nearly choked him. Meanwhile, Caleb grabbed the shield with both hands, shoved the man backwards, and stepped on his foot. The guard tumbled to the ground and Caleb swung the shield around to his back just as a rain of bullets was fired in his direction.

Another fifteen feet and he was out the door. But the chase was far from over. His pulse was pounding in his ears. His eyes scanned for possible escape routes as he ran down the front steps, still holding the armored shield over his back. But the civilians in front of him, on their way to lunch, would be his best safeguard right now. Suddenly he heard the telltale sounds of a motorcycle coming from the east. Almost without thinking, he flung the shield out into the street, which was still a good fifteen feet in front of him. Men and women around him in the plaza scattered like anxious birds. The motorcycle came around the east corner but skidded to a stop at the sight of the new impediment in the road. Caleb hauled the young man off easily, leaped on in his place, and sped off.

FUGITIVE

They would be on his tail. They would be commandeering traffic cams all over the city, freezing his credit cards, and alerting all police units. He needed to get off the streets and to ditch the bike as soon as possible. He headed toward the other side of the tracks as soon as he could. That was one good thing about his undercover assignments: he knew cheapside like the back of his hand.

It wasn't that difficult to stash his bike and exchange his jacket for a hoodie. They hadn't returned his cell phone to him so he didn't have to worry about them tracking him that way. No, he was out of sight from the government for now. The real dicey part was coming up. And if he failed now, his only Plan B was to go back to the tracks and hurl himself in front of the next oncoming train. This had to work.

He knew the place well enough. The only reason he had ever met Bradshaw in public was so the old coot wouldn't get spooked that a G-man knew his hangouts, and disappear altogether. And that's exactly what would happen if this went down wrong. Caleb only had one shot at this. He pulled his hood up, slouched up against a building, across the alley, and waited. Hours slipped by and still he did not move. They would be searching for him, now. Their traffic cams had probably followed his bike into cheapside, but that would be the extent of their digital tracking abilities. There were no working cameras a block past the tracks. If they wanted him, they would have to search grid by grid. And that would take time.

Dusk slowly descended over the city and this deceptively quiet little neighborhood of rundown buildings slowly came to life. Residents who had confined themselves to indoors during the day seemed to grow bolder in the coming darkness, and even stopped to chat in the streets. Bits of wood and old junk was tossed into old fuel barrels and then lit on fire to compensate for the non-existent street lights. No one paid much heed to the stranger hunched up in the alley. Caleb knew how to go unnoticed in this part of town. His attention remained fixed on the door across the alley.

Finally, as the first stars were appearing in the sky, it opened, and a shadowy figure staggered out. Caleb would have recognized Bradshaw's profile anywhere. He darted across the alley, cupped a hand around the man's mouth, and dragged him back into the shadows of the alley and away from the flickering flames of the barrel-fires. Bradshaw huffed for a few moments, but his hoarse voice wouldn't have traveled far even without the impediment of Caleb's hand.

"It's me, it's Weiss," Caleb hissed at him.

This seemed to calm the older man down for a moment, but Caleb knew it wouldn't last long without explanation. He took his hand off the man's mouth and pulled his shoulders around. Bradshaw squinted at him.

"I didn't think you'd come for me yourself. Are you here to kill me?"

"No, I'm not here to kill you," Caleb whispered. "As a rule, I wouldn't trust you with a fiver...but there was so much liquor on your breath that night that I figure you couldn't have been in your right mind, now could you?"

Bradshaw looked him up and down as if he couldn't believe he would get off so easy. "Then you're here to take me for all I'm worth. Aiiee, I've done it now." Bradshaw ran a hand over his head anxiously. "I thought I was in deep before, but now I've betrayed a G-man I may as well have sold my soul to the devil." He peeled off his olive-green beanie and hurled it at the ground, stomping on top of it for good measure.

Caleb, though perturbed by this uncharacteristic behavior, would not be deterred. He grabbed the older man's arm to focus him. "I need you to listen to me, you crazy old man, or this might be the last night of both our lives. "How long have we known each other?"

"You think I keep track of things like that? What am I your girlfriend?"

"How long have I been badgering the life out of you?"

"Two years, I'd say."

"And how many opportunities did you take to spout your anti-government sentiment at me?"

"Every chance I got, I reckon."

"Well, maybe you missed your calling, cause if you'd been a missionary, I'd consider myself converted."

Bradshaw squinted at him, "You trying to preach religion at me?"

Caleb rolled his eyes, "Get me another meeting with the League."

"Ah, geez, now I know you're off your rocker. Aren't you supposed to be dead from the first one?"

Caleb grabbed Bradshaw's collar and shoved him up against the wall, desperation in every feature of his face, "The government took everything from me, do you understand? I gave them my life, my service, and they took everything from me."

Bradshaw's eyes seemed to clear, 'That's what they do, lad. This government's so fat with the blood of innocents it won't be able to hold its own weight much longer."

"Then let me be a part in taking it down." Caleb felt a new passion rising within him. "I'm the G-man, remember? I know their secrets, their strategies. I can be of use to the League."

"Would you put me down, so I can think clearly?"

Caleb complied reluctantly, the anger seeping out of him.

Bradshaw straightened his shirt and jacket self-consciously. "If I had a nickel for every time you shoved me up against a wall...well, we wouldn't be in this situation, would we?"

Caleb slumped against the wall himself and slid down to a seated position, discouragement beginning to weigh on his shoulders. "What am I doing? Why would the League even listen to me? They'll just think I'm a mole."

"It wouldn't be the first time," Bradshaw said.

"The undercovers will find me before daybreak and I'll be sentenced to death."

"Why, what'd you do?"

"Assaulted a superior."

Bradshaw whistled.

"And a dozen guards."

"Now what'd you do that for? Aren't you happy to have a second chance at life after that nasty incident with the League?"

"You weren't the only one who thought I was dead. They wiped my family. My wife will never remember who I am...Believe it or not, I didn't become a G-man with full disclosure of what it would entail."

"That I believe."

"I just wanted to serve my country," a dark despair was settling over Caleb. "Then they put me here, spying on my own countrymen...they memory treated my wife."

His hand instinctively reached for his dog tags where their wedding rings usually hung. But he had lost them in the scuffle with the League. The government would never give them back now. The loss hit him hard.

"They said it was all for my own good, only I'm starting to question that now. I've seen too much behind the scenes. It makes me wonder if they've told the truth about anything..."

Bradshaw clapped a hand on Caleb's shoulder suddenly. "I knew I was right about you. But you sure scared me there for a while."

"What are you going on about?" Caleb asked dejectedly.

"They said you'd never turn, but I said you were too honest a man to stomach the inner workings of the government for long."

Caleb looked up at his companion with glassy eyes. Bradshaw was beaming down on him. Something about him had changed. He was the same man, and yet different.

Bradshaw knelt in front of him, his hand still on Caleb's shoulder.

"You wanted a hearing with the League? You got one. I am the League."

Something stirred in Caleb's gut. "What are you talking about?"

Bradshaw gave a low whistle and a dozen men popped out of the shadows, as if out of nowhere, making Caleb start. He looked sharply at Bradshaw.

"You're their leader?"

"One of them. We believe there is wisdom in numbers."

Anger and confusion washed over Caleb. "So why arrange the meeting the other day? Was it just a trap to kill me?"

Bradshaw winced, "Sort of. The man so eager to shoot you was a mole. You kept pushing for a meeting. We brought you in, hoping he'd react and confirm our suspicions."

"So, I was bait?"

"To be fair, Caleb, you weren't giving me much else to work with. I wanted to try and bring you in, but you put up such a tough front that all the others voted against it."

Caleb was dumbstruck. Bradshaw gave him a hand up.

"Come on. Let's get you off the streets."

"Bradshaw...my wife." Fear suddenly gripped Caleb's stomach. "Do you think they'll use her against me?"

"Oh, undoubtedly. That's why we've taken her somewhere safe. We can't return what was lost. But we can keep her safe...and maybe, one day, you can rebuild your relationship with her."

"H-how?" All the emotions from the last couple hours were beginning to exhaust him.

"I told you, Caleb, I've been watching you. One of my people saw you stumble back into the city like a zombie. We knew what would happen, then. We had your wife and her parents secured before you even got back to your headquarters."

"I don't understand," Caleb stammered, "All that for one man?"

"All that for every citizen in this city," Bradshaw replied solemnly. "You've been looking around and slowly becoming aware of all the evil being committed by the government. What you didn't ask yourself, was why isn't there more of it? Why isn't it more widespread?" His eyes grew moist. "We have been fighting it every step of the way."

The truth hit Caleb with the force of a hammer and he was horrified. "I've been fighting the wrong war."

"I know," his friend said compassionately. "But not anymore."

SHADOW FIGURE

The Light Behind Shadows Part 2

CAPTURED

Sarah Johnson woke up sad.

She couldn't remember what she had been dreaming, but that only made things worse. She had lost something, and now she would never be able to remember what it was.

She pulled the blankets more tightly around her, watching the morning sunlight dance across her fingers. Her mother was preparing breakfast in the kitchen. Her father would be reading the news and muttering disapprovingly into his coffee. They would both smile fondly at her when she emerged from her room, but there would be a strain in their eyes. It was always there, even if they never spoke about it and she never understood it. Today she wasn't sure she was strong enough to face it.

A crash sounded at the front door, making her bolt upright in her bed. Footsteps pounded into the living room, accompanied by harsh voices. Her mother screamed.

Sarah leaped out of bed, grabbed the first thing she could find, and rushed out the door just in time to see her mother collapse. Strange men in tattered clothing filled the apartment. They wore bandanas around their faces. If she didn't know any better, she would have thought they'd just been invaded by a homeless army. Sarah hurled the small mirror in her hand at the man leaning over her unconscious mother. It bounced off of him without effect. Strong hands grabbed her from behind, pinning her arms to her side and covering her mouth. Fumes filled her mouth and nose, blacking out her vision in seconds and sending her back to sleep.

~

She awoke with a headache. She was laying on a lumpy mattress. Fear lanced through her body when her eyes fell on the dull cement wall. She rolled over quickly.

She was in a small room. Her mattress lay directly on the cold floor. The only other furniture in the room was a table with two chairs. A pitcher full of water sat on top. There were no windows, but the far wall had a large dark mirror set into it.

Sarah swallowed her panic and crossed the room to try the door. It didn't budge. She took a deep breath then began rattling the doorknob furiously, finally giving a kick in frustration. There was no getting out. She was at the mercy of her captors—whoever they were. The panic was growing inside of her and she couldn't stop it. She curled up on the mattress, clutching her legs as her breathing grew shallow and rapid. Tears blurred her vision, watering her pillow. She felt as though her life force was bleeding out with them, but she couldn't stop it. A woman entered the room and knelt over her. Sarah's mind was growing fuzzy.

"It's going to be okay," the woman said. "No one's going to hurt you."

A needle pierced Sarah's skin and she slowly drifted back to sleep as the strange woman's fingers brushed back her hair.

~

The next time Sarah woke she was not alone. The woman was there again. She sat in one of the chairs at the table, reading a magazine. Her brown hair was streaked in silver and cinched back in a messy bun. She was short and stocky, but moved with strength and confidence. Her left eye was discolored and surrounded by jagged scar tissue. This seemed to confirm Sarah's worst fears: she was with the terrorists.

All of her fear came back, but this time it pooled in her stomach instead of her chest cavity. She held it at bay by not moving for several minutes, trying to trick her brain into thinking she might still be asleep.

"You're awake," her companion said suddenly.

Sarah flinched and her heart rate spiked. She licked her lips and summoned all of her courage. "Where are my parents?"

"They're safe."

"What are you going to do to them?" Tears sprung forth unexpectedly, but Sarah wiped them away determinedly, sitting up and wrapping her arms around her legs.

"Nothing," the woman answered, leaning forward with a gentle frown on her face. "We have no intention of hurting any of you."

"You expect me to believe that?" Sarah raised her chin slightly in defiance.

The woman picked up a plate of food, set it by Sarah's mattress, then lowered herself to the floor with a sigh. "I know this must be frightening for you. There are a lot of things you don't understand. But you are far safer now than you have ever been. You'll see. We'll earn your trust, no matter how long it takes."

"You mean you'll brainwash me." Sarah made no move to touch the food.

The woman sighed. "No. Your mind is yours and you are free to draw your own conclusions."

"Why am I here? What do you want with me?"

"You and your parents were in great danger."

"From who?" Sarah's voice was beginning to rise.

The woman pressed her lips together. "From the government."

Sarah snorted. "You're crazy. Why would the government want to hurt me? I'm an upstanding citizen. I'm just a teacher!"

The woman's mouth flattened out and a heavy frown wrinkled her forehead.

"I'm not important," Sarah pleaded. "I don't even know where I am. You can drug me again and drop me off somewhere and I wouldn't be able to tell them anything!"

"We can't do that."

"Why not?!"

The woman sighed again. "You need to eat."

Sarah seized the plate and hurled it across the room.

The woman glanced at the dark mirror. She rose slowly to her feet. "You may want to change your mind about eating. It'd be a shame if you were too weak to see your parents at the end of the week." She left the room.

CONVERSATIONS

The days passed slowly for Sarah. She decided the risk of being drugged through her food was worth being able to see her parents and dutifully ate whatever was brought to her. It was simple and bland compared to what she was used to: gruel for breakfast, beans and crusty bread for lunch, and an overcooked potato and canned meat for dinner. After the first two meals she waited anxiously for any sort of physiological change: a decrease in mental acuity, an increase in heart rate, or full on hallucinations. But all of her vital signs remained within the normal range of someone under stress and she grudgingly admitted that if they had done something to her she probably wouldn't notice it until something major happened.

Her companion, whose name was Leslie, visited her every day. The first time she brought books Sarah eyed them suspiciously, wondering what kind of propaganda they contained. But they were books very familiar to Sarah—ones she often used in her classroom. Their presence brought a sense of familiarity into her life which she was not ungrateful for, even if she never thanked Leslie.

They also brought memories of her students and the life she had lived before. She wondered what was happening in the city. Had a search been made for her? How many people had the terrorists taken? What did they possibly hope to accomplish? Though she began to grow accustomed to her new solitary life, she could never be quite comfortable. True to Leslie's word, nobody had harmed her yet. But well-intentioned people didn't kidnap families and hold them prisoner.

After a week, she was permitted to see her parents through a glass partition. They were whole and unharmed. All three of them wept openly when they saw each other, pressing their palms desperately against the glass as if desire alone could eliminate it. The visit did not last long enough. It both eased Sarah's mind and disturbed it. To see them alive and well was a relief, but it also solidified the truth that they were prisoners here too and she had no control over their future.

Leslie persistently tried to engage her in conversation, and as long as the topics stayed away from politics, Sarah grew more and more willing. They talked about childhood memories, cooking, and funny stories from Sarah's classroom. Leslie was patient, kind, and seemed reasonable. Sarah soon began to suspect that perhaps her new friend was not evil, had been brainwashed by her superiors and really didn't know any better. Maybe if she showed Leslie compassion and gained her trust, she could help her see reason.

One day Leslie appeared with a series of crude crayon drawings.

"My son drew these for you." She smiled. "He asked me the other day if you had pictures on your wall. When I said no he was determined to remedy the situation."

Sarah smiled in genuine pleasure. "I didn't know you had a son! How old is he?"

"Seven."

"I love that age," Sarah said. "What's his name?"

"Paulo."

Sarah tried to keep her voice even. "And he lives here with you?"

Leslie eyed her thoughtfully. "Yes. He decorates our walls with pictures."

Sarah struggled to push down the questions that leapt to her tongue. "Children are resilient," she said finally, ducking her head.

"You think it's a poor life for a child." Leslie read her thoughts.

Sarah's head popped up guiltily.

"Sometimes I wish I could give him a better life."

"I'm sure you do your best," Sarah said quickly, even though her heart accused her of lying.

Leslie smiled sadly. "His father was in the Senate. Senator George Vasquez."

The name sounded vaguely familiar to Sarah.

"My husband was so proud when he was elected Senator. He had so many plans for how to make people's lives better. Those first two years were some of the happiest of our lives. He was working his dream job, and after years of fertility treatments, I finally got pregnant. Things changed after Paulo's birth. George got a promotion. I was so exhausted caring for him that it took me longer than it should have to realize something was wrong."

Sarah fiddled with the papers in her hand. She could already imagine how the story ended. This sweet woman's husband had dragged her down and drawn her into this life.

Leslie continued. "He hardly slept anymore. He seemed to be anxious all the time. Sometimes I felt sure he wanted to tell me something but he never seemed able to get the words out. One night he couldn't take it anymore. When he came home his face was so pale. He turned the whole apartment upside down—said he was afraid someone was listening.

"He told me our government was corrupt—that they did whatever they wanted and only pretended to be accountable to the people. He couldn't pretend to play along anymore. He was going to try to stop it, but he was afraid that they would hurt us. He took me and the baby to an abandoned building on the other side of the tracks. I thought he had lost his mind, but I was afraid to contradict him. I didn't know what to do."

"You must have been so scared," Sarah whispered.

"I was more scared the next day when I heard George had been killed in a freak accident. They said he had a heart attack while he was swimming at the gym."

"I heard about that in the news," Sarah mumbled.

"George didn't swim. He was allergic to chlorine." Leslie's eyes had grown red. "The same day there was a gas leak in our apartment building. Half the building exploded, including our apartment."

Sarah's chest tightened.

"My husband knew too much, and our government killed him because he was a good man."

Sarah swallowed. "I am so sorry for your loss, Leslie. But how can you be so sure what really happened?"

Leslie smiled sadly. "My story is not unique, Sarah. There is a point where coincidence adds up to evidence. There are too many inconsistencies in the stories our government tells us—too many people who have gone missing as soon as they began to question."

Sarah pressed her lips together and clenched her fists in her lap. Was it a lie? Could this woman be so cold that she would put on a dramatic performance? No. It was more likely that Leslie really believed it. And if she really believed it, Sarah couldn't fault her for hating the government. But there had to be more to the story.

If there really was some sort of giant federal conspiracy, she would have seen signs of it, wouldn't she? She had not been raised to be gullible. Sarah closed her eyes. It was frustrating to realize that the people who had committed such terrible acts, who she had always believed to be her enemies might be human and have reasons for the things they did. It didn't justify their actions, but it sure complicated the matter.

She picked up the drawings again to try and change the subject. Paulo had drawn her some of his favorite things: firefighters, his pet plant named Howard, and a star chart. The last picture was of a man with his hands on his hips and a grim look of determination on his face. Two words were written underneath: Shadow Figure.

"Who's this?" Sarah asked. "His favorite superhero?"

"No," Leslie said with a peculiar look on her face. "He's a friend of ours."

"He's got a strange name," Sarah said.

"It's a code name. We all use them."

Sarah put the paper down, suddenly uncomfortable.

"He's a good man," Leslie said.

Sarah forced a smile and fixed her eyes on her fingers.

"I think I've overstayed my welcome. You'd like to be left alone." Leslie stood. "I'll tell Paulo you liked his pictures." Leslie gave a knock at the door and it cracked open. They always seemed to know it was Leslie, which meant they either had a camera in the room or that dark mirror was really glass. Sarah was left alone in her cement chamber. After hanging

Paulo's art on the wall with the tape Leslie had left, Sarah began her customary paces about the room.

Five paces to the crack in the wall which reminded her of an old tree. Turn left. Four paces which took her in front of the questionable mirror. She always trailed her fingers along the smooth, cold surface—so different from anything else in the room. Five paces back toward her bed, past the door that only opened for Leslie. Left again, past her lumpy mattress. The rhythm was comforting to her, engaging her muscles and allowing her mind to roam. It was the only time of the day she felt free. But she never completed more than ten circuits at a time.

Inevitably, her thoughts turned to her parents as they always did and she lost her stomach for pacing. What was the point? Even if they let her see her parents once every month, what kind of existence was that? Could she really live like this—shut up like an animal in a cage with no real purpose? Sarah fell into a sort of malaise, sitting on her mattress, fiddling with her necklace. Her eyes stared off into space.

FLIGHT

The door flung open unexpectedly, making Sarah jump. Leslie rushed in. Her face was drawn and tight and for the first time she had a weapon strapped to her belt. She shoved a pair of boots at Sarah.

"Put these on."

Sarah's heart rate rose and her stomach clenched. She was reminded of the morning she and her parents had been abducted and her first instinct was to push back against the suffocating tension that had entered the room. This place might be her prison, but at least she learned what to expect here.

"What's going on?" she asked, setting the boots down on the floor.

"We've been discovered." Leslie's voice was stressed but not panicked. "We need to get out."

Sarah dropped her eyes. Fear and hope collided violently within her.

Leslie knelt and took her face in her hands. "Sarah, I need you to listen to me. It is very important that you do exactly as I say. This is not a rescue mission for them. The tactical team coming will shoot before asking questions. Look at me. Promise me you won't do anything stupid."

Sarah swallowed. Stupid sounded awfully good compared to the depressing future she had just been contemplating. But Leslie's eyes were so sincere and her fear for Sarah's safety was very real. Sarah couldn't help but nod.

The building shuddered and the lights flickered. Leslie jumped to her feet and pulled her sidearm. Sarah stuffed her feet into the boots and stood, instinctively looking around her, but there was nothing here worth bringing along. Leslie grabbed her arm and pulled her through the door.

The corridor looked much the same as her tiny cell—dull cement with no embellishments, only broken up by rusty piping. But simply being in a new space was like a breath of fresh air, and hope soared even higher in her chest. Leslie, though a full head shorter, hauled Sarah down the corridor with considerable strength. Three men and women rushed by them in the opposite direction, nearly bowling them over. The lights flickered out and ear splitting cracks filtered through the thick cement walls.

Leslie hauled open a manhole cover, exposing a ladder. She beckoned to Sarah, keeping a close eye on the dark corridor behind them. Sarah lowered herself cautiously onto the top rungs of the ladder. A breath of cold air came up to meet her. The bars were cold and covered in condensation. How far was the drop?

Maybe it was an abyss. One sloppy misstep could send her plummeting.

"Faster!" Leslie called from above.

Her voice echoed in the darkness, sending Sarah's pulse pounding through her ears. She swallowed the lump in her throat and lowered her feet one at a time, always holding on with one hand. Just as her arms were getting thoroughly tired and she was beginning to fear that falling was inevitable, her boots splashed onto solid ground. She released the ladder and stumbled back, losing her balance and landing in a slimy pool. Leslie caught up in a second, dropping the last foot to the ground. She had a small light on her wristband. She held a hand out to Sarah, pulled her up, and they broke back into a run.

Sarah felt like her insides were on fire. She was thoroughly disoriented and completely filthy. But resolve had hardened inside of her. They rounded a corner, entering an auxiliary tunnel with a little more light. When they raced past a ladder, Sarah made her move. She broke free of Leslie's grasp, sprinted back toward the ladder, and began scrambling up.

"Sarah, no! Come back!"

Sarah shut out Leslie's voice and focused on the rhythm of her pounding heart and ragged breathing. This might be her only chance. And if she could get out, maybe she could help her parents. She reached the top of the ladder and pushed up against the man hole cover. It didn't move.

"No, no, no!" She funneled her panic into her next blow and the manhole budged. Leslie was clambering up the ladder behind her. Sarah pounded the bottom of her fist against the manhole. It broke free and she shoved it aside. Light poured through, giving her renewed strength. She hauled herself up and rolled out onto the street. She struggled to her knees, trying to silence her pounding heartbeat and listen for danger. But the street seemed empty.

Sarah scrambled to her feet and took off running, not even caring what direction she took. Clouds hung low over the city and fog blew around the corners, trapping her in a surreal maze of unfamiliar streets. Her breath puffed out in streams behind her. Had the city been abandoned? Fifty feet later she heard the rapid fire of guns and after a moment's hesitation, ran straight toward it. Leslie chased after her. Sarah rounded a corner and spotted three shadowy soldiers through the shifting fog.

THE SHADOW FIGURE

"Help!" She cried. "Please help me!"

They turned toward her, weapons at the ready. "Hold it right there! Don't come any closer!"

She held her hands up. "My name is Sarah Johnson! I've been kidnapped by the terrorists. You have to help me!" When had she started crying? Leslie was gaining on her from behind. The men lowered their weapons for a moment and whispered among themselves. Sarah stumbled forward. The man in the middle raised his weapon and fired. Leslie threw herself in front of Sarah.

Sarah screamed, catching Leslie's limp body as she fell. A bloody circle was expanding on her friend's chest. Sarah touched it with trembling fingers. It was warm and thick, draining from Leslie's body as fast as a river. There was no stopping it. The clouds released a barrage of half frozen rain, stinging Sarah's skin and turning her nose red. Pain and frustration were building up in her so quickly she feared her heart was about to explode. She let out a cry of anguish, which started low and increased steadily in pitch and volume. Everything was wrong.

The three men were approaching, guns raised. Black spots crept into the peripherals of Sarah's vision as she realized she was about to die. Three shots fired. Sarah closed her eyes and collapsed against the wall, but she did not stop breathing. There was no wound. Her eyes flickered open again. The three soldiers lay dead on the pavement, the strange fog blowing right over them like a parade of ghosts coming to collect their spirits. A strange man was stooping over the bodies, collecting their ammunition. He looked at Sarah and raw emotion filled his eyes. An electric shiver went down her spine.

She tried to move, but her muscles seized up. He sprinted over in a crouch, checked Leslie's pulse, and hauled Sarah to her feet. She cringed away from him, her face covered in snot and tears. He had every right to hit her. Instead he pulled up the hem of his t-shirt and wiped her face. It was unorthodox and yet somehow familiar. Someone had done that for her before. He grabbed the back of her belt and propelled her around the corner.

"Leslie!" The name slipped out of her mouth before she even realized it.

"She's dead," the man said flatly.

Sarah stifled a sob.

They started to round a corner, but the man pulled her back suddenly and pressed her against the wall. She heard shouts and footsteps and her breath froze in her lungs. A few more seconds and the voices faded away again. Night was beginning to fall, turning the fog from white to gray. The temperature was dropping. Her new companion turned his chin toward the radio on his shoulder and pressed a button.

"This is Shadow Figure. Serenity is down, but I've picked up her package. We are on delivery."

He peeled off his hooded jacket and threw it over her, helping her pull her arms through the sleeves, and zipping it up for her as if she was a child. It smelled warm and musky—like a pleasant dream she had once had. "Keep your head down." He paused for a moment, studying the walls of the alley until his eyes landed on one particular symbol. "You see this? If we get separated, you follow the graffiti and ask for a man called Bradshaw, understand?"

She nodded.

"You go to the feds, they'll kill you. Do you believe that now?"

Sarah nodded again. She wasn't sure what she believed, but she couldn't think anymore. Leslie had never hurt her and there was something about this man that made her want to trust him. It wasn't just because he had saved her life. If he threatened her right now she would still trust him. The world was in chaos, Leslie was dead, she didn't know where her parents were, but this strange man with gentle eyes was safe.

The man called Shadow Figure led her through a maze of dark, shabby streets whose residents quickly closed their doors at the sight of them. Federal troops were still lurking here and there, but for the most part they were retreating, uneasy of lingering in enemy territory too long after the sun went down. Her guide seemed to be on much more friendly terms with the shadows.

After a long hour of climbing over trash heaps, ducking under homemade clotheslines, and sloshing through soggy puddles, a strange signal sounded from Shadow Figure's radio. He stepped aside and exchanged a few words that sounded like gibberish then crouched as if waiting for something. She leaned against the wall, panting with fatigue and emotion, and tried to shut out reality by closing her eyes. All sounds of life seemed far away; silence hung heavy around them as if they were cut off from the rest of the world. Twice she got the strange feeling that he was about to speak to her, but he never did. Somehow she knew this was out of consideration to her.

Finally a rusty old van with high suspension and a crooked bumper pulled to a stop in front of them. Its headlights illuminated the swirling fog. The Shadow Figure hopped up to open the door for her. She climbed in willingly enough and he climbed in after her, closing the door firmly. She never remembered the rest of that drive except that, at the end of it, she was escorted into a large building, across a cracked marble floor, and into a room where a sleeping bag had been laid on the floor. She collapsed on top of it and was asleep in seconds.

TURNING POINT

Sarah woke with dry eyes and an aching heart. Sunlight was peeking through the window and dancing on her face. She closed her eyes rebelliously and clung to the last remnants of sleep, hoping to keep the memories from yesterday buried in a dreamy fog. She didn't move. To move would be to accept reality, and she wasn't sure she was ready to do that ever again. Apparently her body wasn't completely prepared to surrender to inertia and entropy. Her stomach began to rumble. She ignored it at first, but it quickly became more insistent. She stirred with a sigh and crawled to her feet.

At least there appeared to be windows here, and the doors weren't locked. The one in front of her hung crooked on its hinges, half-rotted. She pushed it aside and stepped into the hallway. What a strange building. The architecture reminded her of the ancient buildings in her textbooks. But those had all been burned to the ground in the great fire, the new city rebuilt on top of it. Where was she? Some sort of morbid reconstruction? She stumbled down the hallway towards the sound of soft voices.

She emerged into a large marble rotunda, littered with crates, ammunition, and other supplies. A circle of about a dozen men and women halted their conversation and looked up at her. Her eyes gravitated naturally to the only face she knew: the Shadow Figure. Her gaze seemed to make him uncomfortable. He looked at his feet. But all of the other men and women kept glancing in his direction. One of the women picked up two cans and stepped forward.

"I'm afraid we don't have much in the way of breakfast, but it will fill your stomach." She smiled, holding up the two cans. "Chicken soup or canned corn?"

Sarah reached for the corn.

"Good choice," the woman smiled. She put a hand on Sarah's back and led her gently across the room. "Why don't you sit down over here and I'll get you some water?"

She seated Sarah against the wall, rummaged through the supplies and returned with a spoon and a canteen of water. She stooped and opened Sarah's can. "My name is Priscilla. That man over there who looks like a handsome boulder is my husband, Aqui."

Sarah smiled slightly at the description of the large man.

"You need anything at all, you tell us," Priscilla said.

Sarah was holding the spoon in her hand, but her eyes were locked on her blood-stained fingers.

"Are you all right?" Priscilla asked.

Sarah propped her head against the wall behind her and lifted her eyes to the ceiling. Tears slipped down her cheeks.

"I didn't mean to get her killed."

Priscilla pressed her lips together. "Of course you didn't."

"I didn't ask her to come after me! The risk should have been mine."

Priscilla touched her arm. "Sarah, listen to me. Leslie knew what she was doing."

"No, she didn't. Why would anybody do that for a stranger?"

Priscilla took Sarah's face in her hands. "You're not a stranger, Sarah. You're family."

"She had a son. He was her family. Why would she choose me over him?"

"She chose you both, over herself," Priscilla said.

"Why would she help keep me prisoner and then take a bullet for me?! It doesn't make any sense!"

Priscilla pulled Sarah into her arms. "I know honey. I know. But it will."

Sarah cried until the pressure in her chest released and she could breathe again. Then she pushed back and wiped her eyes, tired of crying.

Priscilla handed her the canteen. "Drink some water and eat your breakfast."

Sarah nodded, taking a long swig of water. Her eyes flickered up and she caught the Shadow Figure staring at her. Something flashed across his face as soon as her eyes met his. Guilt? Pain? Regret? Then he looked away. Priscilla crossed over to talk to him. Sarah spooned cold corn into her mouth and focused on chewing. Her muscles relaxed as her stomach filled and the water cleared her mind. The cold despair of the morning seemed to ease its grip.

Priscilla came back over, this time accompanied by the Shadow Figure.

"Why don't we take a walk? Get some fresh air." Priscilla helped Sarah to her feet, walked her down a flight of stairs and out into a courtyard. A dry fountain sat in the center, cracked and crumbling. Vines tangled up the walls and over some sort of statue. Sunlight bathed the courtyard. Its gentle kiss soothed her soul.

"Where are we?" she asked, taking a seat on a stone bench.

Priscilla and the Shadow Figure sat on a parallel bench just across from her. He clutched it with both hands, like he needed the support.

"We're about a hundred miles into the slums," Priscilla said.

"What are you talking about?" Sarah asked. "The slums aren't that big."

"Truth is defined as that which corresponds with reality, right?" Shadow Figure's voice was incredibly gentle. "You'll find a lot of things the government told us don't actually add up."

Sarah brushed a strand of hair behind her ear. "Leslie said something like that. I think she really believed she was keeping me safe."

"Well, that's what she did, isn't it?" he said. "Those agents fired at you."

Sarah cleared her throat. "Yeah, but I'm not really sure they understood who I was—"

Shadow Figure bit his lip, pulled a piece of paper out of his pocket, and handed it to her. "You've been put on the warrant list in every precinct."

"But that's because I'm with you," she protested. "They must think I joined up willingly."

Shadow Figure stared at his feet.

Priscilla turned to him. "She's trying to figure out who to trust. She needs all the facts."

He swallowed and rubbed his palms across his thighs.

Sarah's heart leapt into her throat, though she couldn't say why.

"The League took you and your parents because you were already on the warrant list," he said.

"But why—"

"Because of me," he said, forcing himself to hold her gaze.

Sarah felt an angry blush spread up her cheeks and she stuttered for words. "What did you do?"

A look of pain crossed his face. "The government implemented a policy for their agents, to minimize the emotional toll of service. Or so they said, but I suspect it benefits them more than the families."

"What are you talking about?"

"When an agent dies, they wipe the memory of his closest family. The League thinks they implemented this policy in part because of what happened to George and Leslie Vasquez. She was the only who suspected foul play."

Sarah frowned and shook her head. "But what does this have to do with me?" Something inside of her was already whispering the answer and it terrified her.

He stared at her, chewing on his bottom lip, then stood suddenly. "I can't do this."

Priscilla stepped aside with him, touching his arm in concern. "Caleb."

Sarah could only hear bits and pieces of their conversation.

"Maybe it's better…" he said. "…start over anyway."

"That's not your decision," Priscilla said.

Sarah stood. "What is going on?" she cried in frustration.

They turned to look at her.

"You said it was your fault my family's on the warrant list!" Sarah's heart was pounding, her mind racing through all the logical explanations.

He wouldn't look at her.

Priscilla put a hand on Shadow Figure's arm and sighed. "He's your husband, sweetheart. Your memory was wiped when he went missing in action."

Sarah froze, her heart on fire and her skin ice cold. "But I've never been—I've never met you before." The words sounded pitiful when she said them aloud. She already knew it was true. She could hear this man's voice echoing from her dreams and it terrified her.

The pain in his eyes felt like a punch to the gut. She fumbled for a distraction or excuse. "But if they wiped my memory, why would they still put me on warrant?"

"Because I wouldn't play by the rules," he said sharply. "I saw their true colors and I couldn't play along anymore. So yes, in case you're wondering, I completely ruined your life. You hated my job. You were miserable when we were married. Now you've lost your memory, your freedom, and you're a wanted criminal. You have every right to hate me and I don't blame you. Excuse me." He marched off, avoiding her eyes.

Sarah was left with her mouth hanging open. How could he just walk away and leave her? If he really was her husband, didn't he see that she needed him now more ever? It wasn't his fault that she couldn't remember, but how could she ever remember without his help?

The cry for him to come back lodged in her throat. She didn't deserve kindness from him. She had allowed herself to be duped her entire life. She had resisted every step of the way and gotten Leslie killed. Another tear slipped out and Sarah brushed it away angrily.

Priscilla took her hands. "Take a deep breath. Your world has turned upside down this past month and it's okay to cry."

"I'm tired of crying," Sarah said with sudden certainty. "I'm tired of being kept in the dark and I'm tired of sitting on the sidelines."

"Then help us!"

Sarah looked like she was about to protest.

"Sarah," Priscilla pleaded, "what your government did to your family…that's what they're doing to the city. The worst part of it is that people don't even know. They're being manipulated and robbed."

"But what can I do? I'm just a teacher."

Priscilla smiled. "Who better than a teacher to fight lies?"

"But I've believed those lies for years! I've been teaching them to my students! And apparently there's a huge portion of my life that I can't even remember. I'm not qualified to teach anybody anything."

"Maybe not yet," Priscilla smiled. "But I've a feeling once you do set on what's true, you won't be able to hold it back. So let's sort it out together."

"I have a lot of questions," Sarah said.

"That's good. I can't promise I have all the answers, but we'll do our best to help you find them."

Sarah closed her eyes, took a deep breath, and focused on the warm kiss of the sun on her face. Her world had been thrown into chaos, but there was a sudden peace in her heart where anxious chaos had reigned for the last few years. Part of her had known for a long time that something was wrong. It had nagged at her, aching like a phantom limb. At least now she could see the wound. Dark storm clouds loomed on the horizon, but Sarah wasn't worried. The sun didn't disappear just because you couldn't see it.

GIFTED

Underground

It had been a golden day. But as soon as the sun set all life seemed to be sucked out of the world, leaving behind a cold dark vacuum, otherwise known as a November night. Spencer turned up his collar mechanically, but he didn't really feel the cold. The adrenaline was still pumping too fast through his veins.

Last week the streets had been alive with the sound of children's voices as trick-or-treaters systematically combed the neighborhoods for sweets. They may as well all have been whisked away, like that movie he saw when he was a kid.

Spencer tried to push the thought out of his mind like it was a joke. People were always talking about how this was a great city to raise a family. Maybe it *had* been five years ago. But the shadows had grown longer since then. Maybe if you were tucked up in a warm house at night with your family you wouldn't notice. Spencer didn't have that luxury.

He caught sight of a passing patrol car and turned his face away, pretending to peruse the merchandise in the nearest store window. Nothing good would happen if they saw the blood on his face. He picked up his pace. His destination wasn't far now, and he wasn't about to risk fate and let himself be waylaid by anything.

After slipping down a grungy alley, Spencer pounded the side of his fist on a rusty door and then waited. A few seconds later it cracked open and a pair of eyes squinted out at him from a dimly lit hallway.

"What do you want, kid?"

"I'm just looking for a little distraction. Curtis sent me," Spencer recited smoothly.

The man on the other side of the door scrutinized Spencer for a few seconds, then held the door open and nodded his head, checking the alley before closing the door firmly behind them both.

"Entrance is twenty." The man, who looked ex-military, held out his hand expectantly, his eyes daring Spencer to argue.

"Twenty?" Spencer willingly poked the beast. "Last month it was fifteen."

"Looks like the last guy went easy on you." The bouncer nodded to Spencer's bruised face before adding coldly, "I won't."

Spencer pulled out his wallet with a grumble and forked over the cash. The bouncer made a point of counting the crumpled bills, then led Spencer down the hallway that he could have navigated himself. Why not let the new help feel important? People didn't notice him so much when they were distracted by themselves.

They took two turns and then descended a flight of stairs. The distant roar of a crowd could be heard long before they came out in the underground arena. The noise sent an unexpected thrill down Spencer's spine, making his hands restless. It had been a long time—not since he'd pounded human flesh, he'd done that earlier this evening—but it had been a long time since he'd done it for an audience. The money was just a bonus. Or sometimes, like tonight, it was a necessity.

They were at the back of a large room that resembled an amphitheater. It descended in tiers, centered around a fifteen foot square stage where two bulky figures, gleaming with sweat, were exchanging blows inside a ring. They were exhausted. It must be the last round. He had judged his timing well. The next match would surely be an open challenge.

A sudden commotion in the crowd drew his attention. A tall black man was chewing out some unfortunate soul who had been foolish enough to try and bend the rules. Spencer ducked his head instinctively, but there was really no point in trying to avoid Dallas Brooks, the ring manager. Maybe Spencer had been hoping that Dallas wouldn't be here tonight.

Vain hope. Those piercing eyes were turning towards him. They narrowed on contact and a low growl escaped the man's throat. He charged through the crowd towards Spencer as innocent bystanders leapt out of the way.

The Albino

Spencer cleared his throat nervously, but he stood his ground, shoved his hands deeper into his pockets, and braced himself for the inevitable onslaught.

"What mutton-brain with a death wish let this scrawny excuse for a street rat into my club?" Dallas shouted.

"Pretty sure his name was Bruce and he let me in for an extra five bucks, which begs the question, how many other black-listers has he let in for a little extra cash?"

Dallas seized Spencer's left ear and twisted purposefully, causing the young man to squirm. The large ring manager hauled him back into the mouth of the corridor, released his ear and gripped his chin.

"You still pretending to be a vigilante?" Dallas asked.

"Are you still pretending to care?"

"Haven't learned to shut your mouth, yet, have you? I was considering giving you your money back after I punted your butt into the alley. But I think I'll just keep it."

"Dallas, listen to me. I need this!"

"You need to get your bones broken?"

"I need the prize money from the open challenge."

Dallas started shaking his head.

"I found them, Dallas! I found them. I just need a little front money to get in, and then I'm going to make everything right."

"How many times do I have to tell you that you are way over your head, kid? Go home."

"Home to what?" Spencer asked bitterly. "They took my family from me, Dallas. You think I care about what happens to me?"

"I care about what happens to you."

"If you care about me, you'll let me find justice in my own way."

"Apparently that's what you've been doing," Dallas referred to the young man's bruised face. "And I suppose I can't stop you from that. But I can stop you from breaking your bones here." Dallas glanced about him with a nervousness that Spencer had never seen before.

"They're my bones to break, and if it gets me a little cash, it's worth it!"

"You have to win to get the cash."

"And I can win, you know I can. Why are you treating me like a stray cat? You've seen me fight!"

"That was almost nine months ago."

"And I've only gotten better."

"Good, that's good. At least I can be confident you can protect yourself, but Spencer I want you out of here and I am not kidding around." Dallas' voice was strained.

"What's going on?" Spencer asked.

The arena lights flickered, making the crowd murmur and stir restlessly. The last fight had ended and two men were wiping the floor vigorously in anticipation of the open challenge to come. But Spencer could have sworn the temperature had dropped, and he didn't seem to be the only one who felt it. A ripple of nervous energy circled the arena and left a foul aroma in its wake. Spencer frowned.

Dallas licked his lips nervously. "Listen, Spencer, things have changed around here. I'm not going to pretend that I know how it happened. Too many small compromises. I will deal with it somehow. But this is not a place for you anymore. And I *will* throw you out of the building."

"Without giving me a chance to make any dough?"

"Yeah, and how you going to do that?"

"The open challenge!" Spencer repeated.

"The challenger's already been chosen," Dallas grumbled.

"What?"

"I told you, things around here have changed—"

A roar went up from the crowd as a figure in a dark robe appeared. Dallas' eyes gravitated towards him as if he had no choice and his breath shortened noticeably.

"Is that a man or a mountain?" Spencer whispered.

"It's neither," Dallas said in a strange voice.

The hooded man towered over everyone else around him, like a shadow amplified against a wall, only he was very much flesh and blood. The bulging muscles on his arms appeared larger than most men's legs.

He marched out to the ring like a monarch with no entourage. The crowd parted on either side of him with surprising speed, almost as if his scowl had driven them out of the way. He slipped under the ropes of the ring, shrugged off his robe and hurled it over his shoulder, fully revealing his massive physique.

The room fell silent. His skin was as pale as snow, as was his ghostly hair, which was braided high off his face, yet still fell between his shoulder blades. Every inch of him looked like he had been carved out of white marble, except his coal black eyes.

"So maybe he's out of my weight class," Spencer exhaled.

"He don't have a legal weight class."

"Then what poor sucker took the challenge against him? Can I at least put money against him?"

"No, you don't understand," Dallas said. "*He* took the open challenge."

"Against who?"

"Our standing champion." Dallas wiped sweat from his forehead as he nodded at the group emerging from a doorway on the other side of the room.

The Champion

The first person Spencer saw was an old man. The second was a little boy. The third was enshrouded in a navy blue robe, but he looked no bigger than Spencer himself, maybe even shorter. If he was standing champion, he wouldn't be for long. He might not be alive for long. Things *had* changed around here.

"I thought you didn't run a butcher shop, Dallas."

"Seems I don't run this place at all, anymore," Dallas said quietly. His grip on Spencer had been loosening, but now he let go of him altogether and seized an employee who was walking by. "Where's that paramedic Smith said was gonna be here?"

"I don't know, sir. I think he's delayed in traffic."

Dallas pursed his lips and swabbed his forehead again. "Save us all. This night is gonna haunt me for the rest of my life."

Spencer heard the uncharacteristic comment, but his eyes were on the blue-robed fighter who was entering the ring. He wanted to see this cocky kid's face. The robe slipped off and was given to the old man and Spencer turned to Dallas in sincere shock.

"This is a joke, right?"

"You should leave, kid. You don't wanna watch this."

"Shut it down, Dallas! She's gonna get murdered out there."

Dallas clenched his jaw.

A woman stood in the ring, having just slipped off her robe and handed it to the old man, who must be her trainer. She looked to be about five foot eight, one hundred forty-five pounds. A featherweight against a heavyweight. She was gazing steadfastly at the white monster across the ring as she limbered up her muscles.

Spencer turned back to his friend. "D, I know you're not okay with this. Are you gonna tell me what's going on?"

"What's going on is a large amount of capital disappeared from my bank account approximately six months ago. Then these men started showing up."

"What kind of men?"

"The kind of men with wealthy backgrounds who wanted fighting experience. They were offering up a prize, win or lose. I thought it was easy money."

"What happened?"

"The first couple fights rolled in the money. But then we realized we had a problem…the fans were getting obsessed."

"That's good for business."

"Nah, Spencer. Discontent is good for business. Curiosity is good for business. Obsession makes bad customers. If you're not leading your customers, they're leading you."

"Whatever that means."

"It means there are strange things going on here, and throughout the city…ever since we got that brand new governor." Dallas cut himself off as if afraid he might say too much.

"Don't be one of those people who blames human nature on mysterious evil forces," Spencer scoffed. "Humans are rotten."

"So maybe they are sometimes," Dallas conceded. "But I'm telling you something else is going on."

"What are you talking about?"

"That albino over there don't have a name or no paperwork. The last two didn't neither. And after making meat of their challengers, they just disappeared, too."

"Disappeared?"

"I'm telling you, there ain't no trace of them. I even had a P.I. try and follow one last time. These guys don't seem to exist except for here in the ring. But we've had record crowds the last eight weeks."

The two fighters moved to the center of the ring where the referee was explaining the rules to them.

"That doesn't make this right! She could get killed in there!"

"I can't stop it," Dallas cried helplessly. "It's part of the contract. No one can interfere. Only the fighters can call it off."

"Why did you sign her on at all?"

"The trainer did the paperwork. I didn't know she was a woman!"

The ref was asking them to tap gloves amicably. Neither seemed inclined to be sportsmanlike. Spencer couldn't see the woman's face, but even from this distance he could see the albino's eyes were filled with unmitigated hatred.

Spencer abandoned his manager friend, who had begun to pace anxiously, and pushed his way through the crowd until he came up beside the trainer. A bell marked the beginning of round one. But how could she even last five minutes?

The Fight

Spencer's keen eyes spotted an arena employee along his chosen route. He nimbly lifted the man's badge on his way by, flashing it at the ring of security that kept the crowd at bay, before slipping up beside the old man.

"Get her out of there!"

The two fighters began circling one another. It was virtually a street fight. Anything was permissible as long as they stayed within the confines of the ring and stopped when the bell rang. Three rounds. Five minutes each.

The old man started at the sound of Spencer's voice. "I can't do that," he said.

"Listen," Spencer said, "I understand desperation. I don't care if you got loan sharks after you, or whatever. This isn't worth it."

The old man scrutinized Spencer curiously. "Your heart is in the right place, son, but—"

"I'll take her place." Spencer's stomach clenched as he said it, knowing full well that this could be the death of him. "You can keep whatever money I earn, I don't care. Just let me step in for her."

"Son, I would take her place if I could. But it wouldn't do any good. This is her fight; she chose it."

Spencer had never been so tempted to hit an old man. He turned his attention back to the fight instead. She was moving around well, dodging her opponent's heavy hammer-hands. But it would only take one unfortunately placed blow to snuff out her life. Spencer had a decision to make. His interference could ruin everything. He may never be able to avenge his family. He might die right here. But he couldn't sit back and do nothing. This wasn't right, and he was going to stop it, no matter what it cost him.

He moved to slip between the ropes of the ring, but a powerful force drove him back, and he could've sworn he heard a bone-chilling growl. The lights in the arena flickered again and the security guards stepped toward him menacingly.

"It's just a misunderstanding." The old man gripped his arm possessively and addressed the guards. "Spencer's with me."

They stepped back.

Spencer blinked dumbly, then looked at the old man. "How did you know my name?"

"You told me."

"No, I didn't."

"I must've met you somewhere. The match has started. There's nothing we can do now, except support her," the man explained.

A chill ran down Spencer's spine and he turned to find Dallas' face in the crowd. What was going on here? The woman let out a cry and he whipped his head around again.

She was starting to take hits. He had just nicked her jaw, making her lose her balance. She recovered well, taking advantage of her momentum, tucking into a roll, and popping back to her feet before he could take advantage of her weakness. She was quick and she seemed to know what she was doing. Maybe there was the smallest chance she might survive this thing.

He studied her face for the first time. She had strong features: a broad forehead, a square chin, and the most determined eyes he had ever seen in his entire life. But would they be enough to match the hatred in front of her?

The albino was jabbing at her persistently and driving her around the ring, but he only used his legs half-heartedly. The woman, on the other hand, had good timing with her kicks. Even in her retreat, she was getting in blows to his side and ribcage. They would add up—if she could last, that is.

But retreating around a ring was no way to fight. She would wear out before him, and one misstep could have her on the ground where he was sure to pummel her. She was in a tough position in general. Their significant height difference meant that her most powerful kicks would have to be body blows. And going in for any type of grab might prove more of an advantage to him than to her. Everything was more of an advantage to him.

"What's the deal, you get money depending on how long she lasts?" Spencer asked the old man.

The old man pursed his lips, but did not answer.

Just then the woman landed a solid kick right above the albino's hip. He went for the grab and she landed a strong right hook to his jaw, attempting to follow it up with a re-enforced elbow. But his powerful hands grabbed hold of her shirt, another one of her disadvantages, and he head-butted her. His aim was a little off and the majority of the impact landed on her nose. Spencer winced as he could almost feel it break.

But she responded much faster than he could have imagined. As blood spilled over her lips, she trapped the giant's leg, seized his arm, and flung her full weight to the side, forcing him to topple. She landed three solid blows to his ribs with her elbow before he grabbed at her. She rolled out of reach nimbly. Smart. It was too early to go for the grapple. He was too fresh. She might have a better chance when he was tired.

The bell rang, marking the end of round one, and thoroughly surprising Spencer. She had survived a full round. But that had mostly to do with luck, didn't it? She returned to their corner where the old man was ready with water and a towel.

"You're doing great, kid," the old man said, helping wipe the blood from her face.

Kid? She had to be around thirty. Of course anyone would look like a kid next to this wrinkled old prune.

"It's broken," she confirmed, wincing at his touch. She didn't seem to have even noticed Spencer.

"We'll deal with that after the fight," the old man reassured her.

It wasn't going to be the only thing that was broken if she kept at it.

"All right, you proved your point," Spencer interrupted. "You fought a mean round with this guy. But you'd better pull out, now. It's not worth it."

The woman looked at Spencer for the first time and her eyebrows furrowed. The old man tugged on her chin gently, pulling her attention back to him.

"You can do this, Amy."

What was this guy smoking? Did he want to get her killed?

"Money's no good if you can't spend it!" Spencer spat angrily.

"I'm not doing it for the money," she replied patiently, taking a sip of water.

"Geez, is your pride really worth getting murdered?"

She rinsed out her mouth and spat into the cup the old man provided her, then bent down to where the little boy was watching her with wide eyes and planted a kiss on his cheek.

"You're rootin' for me, right PJ? I can't do this without you."

Spencer ruffled his hair in frustration. Why was the kid here? He didn't need to see this. She acted like this was a basketball game. These people baffled him. He should just walk away. They seemed fully resolved to their stupid decisions. But something held him rooted to the spot.

Maybe it was the dark eyes of the albino giant, which were still hypnotically fixed on Amy from across the ring. Maybe it was the inexplicable force that had kept him out of the ring five minutes ago. Or maybe a wild, reckless hope had planted deep in the corner of his mind.

Wouldn't it be something if she hung with him the whole time? What if she actually beat him? That was ridiculous. This was going to end in a trip to the hospital. Isn't that why Dallas was so desperate to get an EMT on sight? Spencer crossed his arms and chewed on his lip angrily as the second round started.

Against All Odds

The next five minutes were brutal. Amy's opponent was mad. He charged her like an angry bull, raining blows down on her at a pace that seemed unsustainable. It was all she could do to fend him off. About every thirty seconds he got in a serious hit, which looked like it might finish her. Each time she managed to resurrect herself and fend off the inevitable. But she was sustaining serious injuries.

Spencer winced at every blow. Blood and sweat speckled the floor of the ring and seemed to run down Amy's muscles like a waterfall. Her hair clung to her neck everywhere it had managed to slip free from her ponytail. Her movements spoke clearly of pain and desperation.

It seemed like an eternity until the bell sounded and she came into the corner wheezing. Her eye was already swelling up violently and Spencer suspected two to three ribs were broken. But the old man cupped her head in his hands and chuckled.

"You're doing so good, Amy."

She spit out her mouthguard and uttered something between a laugh and a sob.

"This is it, kid. This is the last round and then we're done. Do you understand?"

"It's going to take everything that I have," she gasped.

"It always does," he said. "But you gotta hang with him."

"No," she said angrily, "I want to take him down. We need to finish this. I should be able to finish this."

"What are you talking about?" Spencer asked angrily. "He's going to kill you out there! He may have already. You need to see a doctor."

She was shaking out her legs and exhaling slowly. "Roscoe, tell me I can do this," she said.

"I have no doubts," the old man replied genuinely.

"PJ, if I do this, will you make me your famous butterscotch pudding?"

The little boy smiled bashfully.

"You've still got that picture in your pocket, right?" She asked.

PJ nodded.

"It hasn't changed, has it?"

He smiled and shook his head.

The bell sounded and the last round began.

Amy fought with a new intensity. The injuries were still there and were apparent in the choices she made. But there was also a passionate recklessness to her attacks that he had never seen before.

No, he *had* seen it before—in his mother, on the day that she died. He had never understood what people meant about 'mama bear syndrome' until he saw his own mother fearlessly take on the drug lords who had sucked the life out of her only daughter. And the only thing that had stopped her from ripping them apart that day was a bullet. The cowards had outnumbered her. Spencer suddenly wondered if Amy was a mother.

He almost felt sorry for this hulk of a man up against her. Aside from the monotonous hatred, his eyes were empty. There was no story behind them. He knew nothing of the weakness and vulnerability that Amy knew, and so he couldn't know real strength, either.

But the albino hadn't fatigued. Far from it. He pounded on as relentlessly as he had from the start. All the strength of Amy's emotions seemed to ricochet off him like water off a rock. Spencer's hope waned. Had she done any damage at all? Would she break herself through her relentless assault? The only thing that comforted him was that somehow, inexplicably, she seemed to be speeding up. In fact, the albino was beginning to look sluggish next to her.

It happened in an instant. She saw her opportunity and landed a high kick directly to his jaw. He stumbled and slipped to one knee. She instantly went in for the grapple, slipped around expertly and landed his massive frame in a rear naked choke. Knowing her injuries and her fatigue, Spencer could hardly believe his eyes.

The albino thrashed and strained, but she was holding on with a vice-like grip. Spencer counted the seconds anxiously and waited for the tap out. But this guy wasn't giving up easily. He fought and strained long after what Spencer would have thought humanly possible. But finally, there it was: submission.

The Storm

Amy released him and a roar filled the arena. Spencer half expected a cheap retaliation, but the pale giant slunk away to his own corner. Amy got to her knees, moving as if all the pain had caught up to her at once. Roscoe and PJ slipped under the ropes and ran toward her as the ref announced her victory over the address system.

Spencer put a hand into the ring tentatively, but when he faced no resistance he leapt over the ropes altogether and bounded to Amy's side. Roscoe was attempting to help her up and she was crying out in pain. Spencer wedged himself gently under her other shoulder and eased her to her feet.

In the room around them, the crowd was frothing with mixed emotions, some angry, some elated. Prime riot conditions. They had to get Amy out of there before something stupid happened. Hopefully Dallas was still boss enough to handle it.

A movement in the opposite corner caught Spencer's attention and he did a double take. Maybe it was just because he was closer now, but he could have sworn the albino had been taller. They reached the edge of the ring and an employee began unlocking the ropes to let them through. Spencer glanced back at the albino and blinked in confusion. The lighting must have changed. He didn't look as pale as before.

"Spencer!" Roscoe called his attention to the stairs and together they began helping Amy to the back of the arena.

Someone called out behind them. Amy turned dutifully, almost as if she had been expecting it. A thirty-something-year-old man climbed up the steps behind them. There was something vaguely familiar about him.

"Good fight." The man offered his hand amicably. "You were a beast out there."

Amy took it with a friendly smile, but her eyes were sad.

The man retreated back the way he had come and Spencer stared after him in confusion until it suddenly clicked. But how was it possible? He turned back to Roscoe and Amy in consternation.

"Was that—how is that? What just happened?"

Roscoe eyed him sharply, but Amy spoke.

"Not here," she said.

"Let's get her to the car," Roscoe agreed firmly.

"The car? She needs to go to the hospital."

"And what would she say when they ask her about her injuries?" Roscoe asked as they continued forward.

"I'm not going to lie," she added.

"She's got some serious injuries," Spencer protested.

"And we'll deal with them the best we can," Roscoe said testily. "This ain't our first rodeo. Now are you gonna be a nuisance or a help? Cause I figure this isn't much your business, anyhow."

Spencer shut his mouth and kept his place beside Amy. He couldn't fully explain why, but it had become important to him to make sure she was safe. They pushed their way through the crowd, with the help of PJ who went before them like a front runner. Dallas paid them little heed for having been so concerned before the match. Spencer would take it up with him later.

They shoved through the door and were met with a frosty bite of air, so cold it would almost be as good as an ice pack if it didn't make your whole body shiver. The night was still and strikingly quiet compared to the cacophony they had just emerged from.

A ghostly wind rattled a few leaves, but the sound was anything but reassuring. In fact, Roscoe's anxiety seemed to have increased tenfold since stepping out the door. He ushered them all to a beaten, old truck like a mother hen and then turned a sharp eye on Spencer.

"I don't suppose you'd mind riding along? I could use your help getting her out at the other end. I ain't as young as I used to be."

Spencer hopped in without hesitation.

Roscoe nodded in satisfaction and then climbed behind the wheel with a stiff groan. They pulled away from the curb and into the deserted streets. Where were all the streetlights? Had they all gone out at the same time?

The ride was quiet, but uneventful. After about ten minutes they pulled into a sleepy little neighborhood with thickly shuttered windows. The pickup crept down the street almost guiltily before crawling to a stop before a dark green house. They all moved about with extra care, making as little noise as possible. Spencer did not have to ask why. Over the last five years it had become second nature to him and everyone else in this city.

It took a bit of maneuvering to get Amy out of the truck, up the drive, and through the front door. But things got better from there. PJ ran ahead and prepared everything with foresight that could have only come from experience.

They took her to the bathroom first, where Roscoe helped her clean off the blood. PJ settled at the kitchen table with a piece of paper and a fist full of crayons. That's when Spencer noticed the drawings, which decorated the place like wallpaper.

He understood the concept of displaying a few pieces of art on the fridge, but this was a little excessive. Who was this kid, Van Gogh? A gust of wind slipped through an open window in the kitchen, threatening to strip the pictures off the wall, and it brought with it the scent of rain.

Questions

Spencer moved quickly to shut the window. Sure enough, it was pouring outside. He hadn't thought to ask if the old man would give him a ride home. He'd cross that bridge when he came to it. The wind began to whip the rain against the window. But the sound of PJ's furious scribbling rose above it, drawing his attention once more. That was it—the poor kid had to draw his feelings. How else was he supposed to cope with what he had just seen?

"Spencer."

Spencer jumped at the sound of his name and looked guiltily toward the bathroom.

Roscoe was watching him. "Would you come here a moment?"

Spencer crossed the room dutifully. Amy looked a good deal better with the blood washed off her face. But her eyes were weary of the pain. He knew that feeling too well.

"Would you help with the wrapping?" Roscoe asked, demonstrating with his hand.

A faint blush touched Spencer's cheeks. "Wouldn't you rather?"

"The arthritis is acting up again," Roscoe said. "Besides, I reckon you know what it feels like to be on the other side." He gestured toward Spencer's face.

"Don't worry, kid." Amy smiled at his hesitation. "You're not my type. And if you get handsy, I got no problems shifting your jaw. Now would you please wrap up my ribcage so I can lay down?"

Spencer cleared his throat and nodded. Roscoe handed him the bandage and Amy managed to lift the clean, loose shirt that had replaced her tank top. Spencer made quick work of it. Roscoe had been right about that—he knew what he was doing. When he was done he helped Amy off the counter and onto the couch.

A peal of thunder sounded overhead and the lights flickered out, somehow amplifying the sound of the rain.

"PJ, come join me on the couch." Amy spoke almost immediately, a hint of anxiety in her tone. No wonder that she'd be a little jumpy after what she'd been through. The little boy darted to her side obediently while Roscoe went to fetch some light.

Spencer shifted his weight. "Do you all live here?"

She only hesitated a moment. "Roscoe's very good at taking in strays."

"I didn't mean to imply—"

"It's all right," Amy said. "We're a different sort of family, I guess. We need each other."

Spencer cleared his throat.

A light suddenly broke through the darkness as the old man returned with a candle.

"Take a seat, son, I think you have some questions."

"I don't even know where to start."

"Well, why don't you try? That'll help me know where to start with the explanations."

"Roscoe, do you think it's a good idea?" Amy asked hesitantly.

"What did you see as we were leaving the arena?" Roscoe asked.

"The other fighter," Spencer began hesitantly, "he changed."

Amy looked surprised.

"Changed how?" Roscoe pressed.

"He was this huge albino guy at the beginning and at the end he was just…ordinary. And don't tell me that I'm crazy. I know what I saw."

"Of course you do. It's just significant that you remember it."

"What?"

"People see what they want to see. Son, there's a war going on in this city. But you've known that for a while now, haven't you?"

Spencer didn't answer.

"The choices people make have consequences, some tangible, some intangible. Just because we can't see them, doesn't mean they aren't real."

"You mean like the local government?"

"And the families. And the business owners. And every citizen in this town. Of course leadership has a great deal of influence and thus holds greater responsibility."

"So what does that have to do with what happened tonight?"

"You've been given a gift, Spencer. Which means you can't be a civilian no more."

Gifted

"What are you talking about?" Spencer's voice was low.

"You don't think Amy jumps into the ring with men twice her weight just for kicks, do you? She won an important battle tonight."

"Against who?"

"Darkness. Evil. Corruption."

"You're telling me that you can physically fight evil in a ring?"

"You don't believe us," Amy said.

"No, you don't understand. I've been doing the same thing!" Spencer stood in his excitement. "Well, sort of. I got to this point where I realized the cops don't know what's going on. Not really. Justice isn't happening out on the streets. We gotta fight for it ourselves. That's why I quit fighting in the ring. The real fights are happening outside the arenas."

"Hold on a second, Spencer."

"No, I'm serious. I'm ready for this. Maybe this is what I've been waiting for, maybe this is what I was meant for. I've never been good at anything else!"

"That's not exactly how it works, son. We don't pick fights based on our own judgment."

"Oh, right. So schedule a fight for me like you did for Amy. I'll take on whoever you ask."

"We don't all have the same gifts, Spencer. Did you see me and PJ out there fighting? Somehow Amy is able to push back the darkness by physically fighting it, but it costs her a great deal."

"I'm not afraid of pain. I can handle it."

"PJ has the gift of foresight and vision. That's what these drawings are for."

"Roscoe's an interpreter," Amy jumped in. "He matches up PJ's pictures with people, places, and times."

"Okay, I still don't see the problem with me helping."

"You don't choose your gift," Amy said. "You only discover it."

"I've been fighting since I was a kid. I have a burden for justice. I'm not afraid to take a hit."

"Your gift isn't fighting," Roscoe said with certainty.

"What makes you so sure?"

"Amy said I'm an interpreter," Roscoe began. "Part of that means I see to the heart of things. The gift is not necessarily the thing that comes most naturally to you. In fact, I have often found that the gift is balanced by weakness. Without my gift, I have a tendency to be critical and judgmental. Believe it or not, Amy struggles with fear. Your gift will not play to your vanity, Spencer. It will challenge you in a way that nothing ever has before, and you'll become a better man because of it."

Spencer clasped and unclasped his hands. "So what's my gift?"

"Do you feel it, Amy?" Roscoe asked.

She frowned in confusion.

"I haven't given you any pain medications."

Her eyes widened in understanding and she looked at Spencer.

"What are you talking about?" he asked.

"Spencer, I believe you have the gift of healing. And you could do a great deal of good with it, if you chose."

A bolt of lightning spilled light through the windows for a split second, quickly followed by the loudest crack of thunder Spencer had ever heard. The storm must be right above them.

"I'll take you wherever you wanna go in the morning, son. But I don't think we should go out in this storm. We've got a spare bedroom if that'd suit you."

Spencer nodded and Roscoe puttered off to make preparations. Another bolt of lightning split the sky. Spencer sat on the other side of PJ and put his head in his hands. PJ got up suddenly and returned to the kitchen table.

"You all right, there?" Amy asked.

Spencer didn't answer.

"It was difficult for me too, at first. I was always the peace maker. I used to avoid conflict at all costs. When Roscoe told me what my gift was, I thought he was crazy."

"I don't see what's so wrong about what I'm doing," he muttered.

"What are you doing, exactly?"

"Drug dealers killed my mom and might as well have killed my sister. They've been wreaking havoc all over this city. Somebody needs to stop them!"

"And you're just the guy for the job, right? Because your hatred for them is justified and they are evil to the core. And if you're on the side of justice, all of your actions must be just, right?"

"What are you getting at?" Spencer snapped.

"How we fight is just as important as what we're fighting for. I'm sorry about your mother and your sister. But there are dark forces beyond just individual people. And until you see that, you won't be able to make much of a difference no matter how hard you try."

Spencer stifled a sob. Where had that come from? Now Amy would think he was an idiot. But the emotions weren't going away. And they clouded his brain.

"I know, it's a lot to take in," Amy said.

The lights flickered back on and a small hand touched Spencer's shoulder, making him start. PJ was standing beside him with a piece of paper. The little boy held it out to him.

When Spencer took it, it became more than a picture. The figures sprung off the page and moved about like he was replaying a memory. He saw his mother at work in the emergency room, intersecting people in the darkest hours of their lives. In this drawing he could see how her kindness had impacted thousands of lives. Trails of golden light dripped from her gentle fingers and kind words, wrapping around broken hearts and planting hope where there had only been darkness.

And then the scene changed and Spencer saw a man he immediately recognized, walking through the streets of the city. This man was also called into situations of heartbreak and hopelessness. He visited a home where a fifteen-year-old boy had been riddled with bullets. The family sat nearby, weeping in desperation, but too afraid to take him to the hospital where either the cops or the rival gang would be waiting.

But the man placed his hand on the boy's chest and a blue light began to radiate from his palm. The dark shadows in the room shrieked with anger and attempted to attack the man. But Amy was fighting in the ring that night. He could see her across town. There were wrinkles around her eyes now, but she was just as determined as ever. And as long as she sweat and bled, the shadows seemed unable to do much damage to the man with his hand on the wounded boy. The blue light seemed to enter the boy and disappear. But a minute later, he woke up.

The images vanished as abruptly as they had appeared and Spencer found himself holding a simple drawing in a worn living room with rain thundering on the glass French doors. He took a moment to catch his breath.

"You saw it, didn't you?" Amy asked. "PJ's vision?"

Spencer turned towards her. "I thought they were just drawings."

"Sometimes they allow us to see what he sees," she explained. "I've only ever seen one. I think Roscoe sees a lot more of them."

Spencer was quiet for a moment. "It was me. It was about the future I could have if I develop my gift."

"And?"

"And you were right. How we fight is just as important as what we're fighting for. But Roscoe was wrong. My gift is fighting. My mother was a fighter, too. But she fought the darkness by spreading light and hope. She was the strongest person I ever knew. Maybe it's time I started fighting by her rules."

Spencer held up his hand. A tiny blue spark began to glow in the palm of his hand. A bolt of lightning struck the tree outside the window and the accompanying thunder was so loud that the house shook. Spencer smiled. Darkness wasn't going to take this city without a fight.

BEAST IN THE MACHINE

It was a quiet village. Isabelle knew it would be. There were only two reasons people moved to Ilford: to get away from society or to work at the world's second-best scientific research center. In Ilford, it wasn't difficult to differentiate between the two. The scientists were middle-aged men with disheveled clothes who barely saw the light of day. The locals were the ones gossiping about them in the open-air cafes. Now they peered curiously at Isabelle and her father as the pair drove by in their sedan. Isabelle stared back openly, fascinated by the open-air buildings that breathed in the fresh ocean air.

The villagers themselves had seen their share of ocean winds and salty storms. The young ones were strong with bright eyes, agile hands, and brown skin. The older ones looked like withered old trees. Though their eyes squinted at her and their mouths turned down in suspicious frowns, Isabelle smiled.

"What a quaint little place," she said to her father as they began unloading boxes into the house.

"I'm glad you like it, dear. I've heard the locals aren't so welcoming to outsiders."

"But did you see the tide pools under that sunset, Papà? I don't think I could ever be unhappy with a view like that; I don't care how nasty our neighbors are. And surely they can't be that bad."

"Well, if *you* can't win them over, love, I'll write them off as not worth knowing." Her father kissed her on the cheek, scratching her with his whiskers, then reached for his hat.

"Are you going somewhere?"

"To the lab."

"But we just arrived," Isabelle protested.

"Dr. Glass said I was to come over as soon as I arrived."

"Well, that seems like a bad precedent, doesn't it?"

"Now, now," her father chastised her gently, "I know that brain of yours. If you could postpone your final analysis of my new boss until you actually meet the man, I'd be much obliged."

"I will try to keep an open mind," Isabelle said, "but I cannot promise to keep my mouth shut."

"Fair enough. Don't do all the unpacking without me."

"I certainly will," Isabelle replied. "You always put everything in the wrong place."

"I do, don't I? Very well then. But don't work too hard. And don't—"

"Unpack your office? I wouldn't dream of it. You can make your little mess all yourself."

"I'll be back in an hour or two," he promised.

She locked the door securely behind him and turned to survey the night's work. She had learned the hard way that with him one to two hours really meant three to four. She may not like it, but there was no fighting it. The best she could do was make the house as comfortable as possible by the time he got back.

It was a small, rather crooked little cottage with a spiral staircase in the center, giving the impression that the small dwelling twisted around itself like a great oak. This was a great relief to Isabelle, who had feared the Institute would set them up in some pre-fabricated box. But she could befriend this house. She just had to earn its trust first. She'd start by giving it a little fresh air. The house must be suffocating; it smelled staler than an old sock. She wove her way through the boxes, wrestled with the latches, and pushed open both the panes and the forest-green shutters.

Crisp, salty air eddied into the room like the first fingers of high tide on a thirsty shore. It carried with it the unmistakable scent of coming rain. Isabelle took a deep breath, tied her hair back in a bandana, and set to work unpacking the kitchen.

A light rain descended on the cottage just as evening fell. Having finished the kitchen, Isabelle moved on to the living room with renewed purpose. The steady rain on the roof kept her company. When she finished, it was nearly ten o'clock and high time to get tea and dinner ready for her father.

But she took a moment to place a gilded picture frame on the mantle. The beautiful woman stared back at her with gentle eyes, so different from the eyes that Isabelle remembered. The mother she had known as a child would have loved this house. Isabelle pushed the thought aside as her chest filled with pain and remorse, and focused on preparing dinner for her father.

Twenty minutes later he burst through the door with familiar enthusiasm, shaking off his umbrella and generally dripping water all over the entryway. His face was beaming.

"How did it go?" Isabelle asked with a grin as she helped him out of his rain boots.

"I'm sorry I'm later than expected. I just couldn't seem to tear myself away. The labs, Isabelle! I've never seen anything like it! Dr. Glass had all the best equipment. He's as eager to get started as I am. And I'm to have my own assistant."

"I'm glad."

"You've been busy," her father said as he entered the kitchen where a tray had been set out for him.

"It's a good start," Isabelle agreed. "I'll finish up tomorrow and then start looking for a job."

A cautionary look entered Mr. Richter's eyes. "Yes, I asked Dr. Glass about that. I thought maybe he could give you some recommendations. There doesn't seem to be much open, and he warned me that your association with me might blacken your resume in the village."

"I'm not sure Dr. Glass is an objective party, Papà. It's a bit too easy to reciprocate prejudice. I am determined to set out tomorrow with an open mind."

~

The rain had vanished by morning, leaving the little seaside village freshly scrubbed. But fog clung to the hills and cliff sides, and dark clouds loomed over the moody ocean, threatening another storm. Isabelle's father was off as soon as light seeped under the windowsills. She spent the first hours of the day setting the house in order before making her first foray into the village. She might as well stock the pantry and begin her job inquiries at the same time.

Tugging on her polka dot rain boots, a charcoal gray, heavy knit sweater, and a slouch beanie, Isabelle descended the driveway and stepped out on the cobblestone streets with optimism. The air smelled of rich earth and a touch of salt. Gulls called back and forth above the fishing boats that bobbed up and down on the tempestuous sea. Directly in front of her, the village was waking up.

"Such a shame," the Grocer mentioned casually as he assisted the customer in front of Isabelle. "I heard a Lab Coat took up residence in the old maple house. They'll be cutting into it soon, I suspect, tearing up the hundred-year woodwork to put in their modern-day contraptions."

"Shame," the woman he was talking to scoffed. "People don't deserve a beautiful house like that if they aren't going to take care of it."

"Why didn't they just move into a townhouse, like the rest of their kind?" someone else chimed in.

Isabelle smiled. "Maybe they believe that a house shouldn't come out of a box but should have history and character."

"Ha! They call it character until the plumbing acts up a bit. Then it becomes inconvenient."

"Poor plumbing does sound a bit inconvenient." Her eyes sparkled good naturedly. "But I don't think it calls for ripping apart something as lovely as Maple House. Maybe we should give these newcomers the benefit of the doubt and see what happens."

The Grocer muttered something under his breath as he began helping her with her purchases.

"Since you've been so helpful," Isabelle continued, "I wonder if I might ask you something. I'd like to find a job. Do you know of anyone looking for help?"

The Grocer grumbled. "Nothing available for you, unless you like mopping up fish guts."

"Well, I'll never know unless I try…"

"It was a figure of speech. There's nothing open on the docks, neither," the Grocer said stubbornly.

"Well, you'll be sure to let me know if you hear of anything? I'm willing to try my hand at 'most anything."

"There may be something available." A woman stepped forward. "One of our foremost families has been looking for help around his estate for some time now."

The Grocer frowned at her. "What are you talking about?"

"They live in that great mansion on top of the cliffs. Surely you've seen it?" the woman continued.

"Sebastian Prince." The Grocer's face lit up mischievously. "She's right. If you're willing to try anything, you ought to go talk to his housekeeper."

Isabelle smiled. "I'll head up there this afternoon. Thank you." She piled up her arms with groceries and made her way back home. The dark clouds from the morning were finally moving in and an icy wind was picking up. Isabelle donned her rain jacket and snatched up a red umbrella before heading out again.

The winks and nods of the begrudging villagers had not been lost on her. She had little doubt that they meant some kind of mischief by sending her up to the Prince estate. But there could be no harm in trying. A fine, misty drizzle dropped in about halfway through the village, raising a muted symphony from the clay tile rooftops and cobblestone streets. The sound became softer, like rain falling on velvet, as she left the village behind and began climbing the hill north of the village to the great estate.

It perched above the black cliffs with solemn dignity. Isabelle had innocently assumed it was another research facility, for even though it sat a good ways apart from the clusters of labs directly east of the village, it resembled them far more than the old-fashioned fishing huts. Carved out of muted, white stone, it stood four stories tall and on closer inspection looked a great deal more like a museum than a house.

But the hike up the hill alone was worth the journey. At the foot of the cliff, the roiling black waves tossed and crashed with a graceful yet ferocious power. Farther out to sea, flocks of birds rode the swells with an elegant dignity, undisturbed by the gentle rain dimpling the water all about them. And when Isabelle turned around, the sleepy village spread out before her like it had been taken straight out of a painting. After a sigh of deep contentment, she ascended the steps to the great house, feeling nearly invincible.

There was no response to her initial knock, so she tried again, putting a little more force into it. A raspy, mechanical noise caught her attention and she looked up to see a camera pointed at her.

"Hello, I'm Isabelle Richter. My father and I have just moved here and I'm looking for work. Someone in the village said you might be hiring?"

Something clicked and the door swung open.

Isabelle stepped forward, prepared to meet her host, but the ornate entryway was completely empty. She passed into the hall, which was paved with marble, and tried not to gawk at the portraits on the wall.

The door hadn't just opened by itself. Someone had let her in.

"Hello?"

There was no response. Then Isabelle heard a soft pitter-patter. She rounded the corner and stopped short in surprise. In front of her stood a tiny robot, no taller than her knee. It had two cylinder shaped legs, a round torso, two spindly little arms, and a round popsicle head with enormous turquoise eyes. An antenna protruded off the top of its head like a thick piece of hair.

"Who are you?" Isabelle asked in amazement.

The little robot tilted its head and blinked.

"I don't suppose you're the butler around here, are you?" she teased.

It turned and began walking back the way it had come, then paused and looked back at her expectantly.

"Am I supposed to follow you?" she asked.

It nodded.

"Well, all right then." This afternoon might turn out far better than she had imagined.

The little robot took her up a magnificent staircase and down a thickly carpeted hallway. On her left, a row of wall-length windows gave her a breathtaking view of the stormy sea. She wouldn't mind working in a place like this.

But the door at the end of the hallway was very different than anything she'd seen so far. It was thick and metallic. The little robot raised one of its spindly little arms to a digital interface and the door popped open with a loud hiss.

"Is the interview to be in here?" Isabelle asked a little timidly.

The robot wiggled its arms enthusiastically and shuffled through the door. She followed after only a slight hesitation.

The room was nearly pitch black. There was just enough light from the open door behind her to reveal the shadowy silhouettes of antique furniture. Even the sound of the rain seemed muted behind the thick, brocade curtains.

Isabelle moved instinctively to the ten foot windows and hauled back the curtains one at a time. It took a deal of effort. Each curtain must have weighed about twenty pounds. But she was immediately rewarded with a soft flood of healthy, spring light and the soothing patter of the rain against the window panes.

"What, in the name of all things holy, do you think you're doing?" a deep voice slurred.

Isabelle whipped around.

About six feet away, a very disheveled man lay sprawled on a sofa. His posture was relaxed, his face grizzled and unkempt, but his dark brown eyes gazed at her with more menace than Isabelle had seen in her entire life. Her heart leapt in fear.

"I've come for an interview," she replied evenly, "but perhaps I've got the wrong room. I certainly didn't mean to disturb you."

He started off the sofa with more power than she could have imagined, the sparks in his eyes heating to a full-fledged fire and forever redefining intensity in her mind.

"Interview?" he snarled at her. "I thought I made it clear last time that you weren't to set foot in this house again."

Isabelle took a single step backwards, ignoring her racing heart. "I actually don't think I've ever been in this house before. Perhaps you've mistaken me for someone else."

He grabbed a side table and upended it forcefully, sending a lamp and two crystal glasses to the floor in a cacophony of shattered glass. But Isabelle also noticed the rapid rise and fall of his chest and the protruding veins on his neck.

Unwanted memories flooded her mind, constricting her chest and making her palms sweaty. She shoved her emotions down with well-practiced determination, crossed her arms deliberately behind her back, and angled her body away from him. When she spoke, her voice was gentle.

"Well, that's one way to communicate, I suppose. But if you were to use words next time, I'd be much more likely to understand what you actually want." Her own words served to calm her racing heart.

The man clenched his fists and raised them to his mouth, pacing back and forth now. But he did not knock anything else over, nor did he yell at her.

A new voice spoke from the doorway. "Sebastian, what's going on? Who is this?" A small matronly woman in a crisp uniform stood in the doorway.

Sebastian turned to her like she was a lifeline. His hands were trembling now. "Get her out of here." He careened past her like a drunken man and disappeared from sight.

The housekeeper turned fierce eyes on Isabelle. "How did you get in the house?"

"I believe I was let in by your butler."

"We don't have a butler," the woman retorted.

"It was a very small robot."

The woman's eyes registered recognition. "Cog?" she called sharply.

The little robot emerged guiltily from behind the sofa, crept over to Isabelle, and took hold of her leg protectively. The housekeeper crossed her arms.

"Well, this is new for you. When did you start letting strangers into the house?" She switched her gaze to Isabelle. "Who are you, exactly?"

"My name's Isabelle Richter." Now that Sebastian had left, her heartbeat was rapidly returning to normal. "I'm looking for work. I was told in the village that you might be interested in hiring me?"

The housekeeper's eyes softened significantly. "I see. Well, I'm sorry to tell you that you were sent up here as part of a cruel joke."

Isabelle's eyes dropped to the carpet. Perhaps she shouldn't be disappointed after the reception she had received, but she was.

"But you've handled yourself surprisingly well," the housekeeper continued. "What is that you said you do?"

Isabelle's eyes returned to the woman's face. She had a sharp nose, but friendly eyes. "I can do a lot of things. But I got my degree in literature and information science."

"Well, we have a library here that is an absolute nightmare. Would you be interested in putting it to rights for us? It can be a contract job for a couple of weeks. We'll see how it works out."

"I would love that," Isabelle began hesitantly, "as long as Mr. Prince doesn't have any objections."

"I manage the household," the housekeeper replied quickly. She extended her hand suddenly. "Mrs. Kettler."

Isabelle took her hand gratefully. "I really appreciate this."

"The villagers can be cruel to newcomers," Mrs. Kettler said. She began leading Isabelle back down the hallway. "Can you start tomorrow?"

"Yes, of course. Am I to work all day?"

"I think mornings should be sufficient, don't you?"

"That's fine."

"Good. We'll see you tomorrow morning at eight o'clock. Do you need a ride home? I'm afraid the storm's still going strong."

"I'm not afraid of a little rain." Isabelle picked up her umbrella. "Goodbye Mrs. Kettler. And thank you."

~

Maple House smelled of pot roast and baked potatoes by the time Dr. Richter came home. The rain had dissipated completely by then, leaving behind a clear night with a lonely wind biting at the windows. But father and daughter were as cozy as could be after dinner, sitting with a cup of tea next to a roaring fire.

Isabelle's father had talked about his work all through dinner, but now it was her turn.

"I have some news," she said as she stared into the dancing flames of the fire. "I got a job today."

"That's wonderful! I knew if anyone could win over these stubborn villagers, it'd be you. Where are you working?"

"Have you seen the great estate on the cliff side?" Isabelle asked.

Dr. Richter paused with his teacup in midair. "The Prince estate?"

"Yes, that's the one. Apparently, they've got a great library that needs to be put in order," Isabelle said.

"Well, of course it's lovely you've found a job," Dr. Richter said. "How did you find the master?"

Isabelle hesitated and then smiled knowingly. "What have you heard?"

"I know he's a recluse, and people become angry when his name is mentioned, but they don't say much."

"To be fair, I only spoke with him for about three minutes."

Dr. Richter raised his eyebrows.

"I'm afraid he was quite rude and angry. I don't think he interacts with people very much."

"Do you think it wise to work for him?" Dr. Richter asked gently.

"I think it's worth a try. The villagers sent me up there expecting me to come back with my tail between my legs. Perhaps there's some value in showing them I'm tougher than I look."

Dr. Richter studied his daughter's face thoughtfully. "You have nothing to prove on that account."

"People always think I'm a pushover at first."

"They'll know different soon enough." His eyes were growing moist. He took her hand. "You're stronger than the lot of them put together."

She squeezed his hand and swallowed the lump in her throat.

"There is no need for you to work in an environment you're not comfortable with," he continued. "You've been through enough."

"Papà, when you received this job, I was happy to move here with you, because I knew what an incredible opportunity it was for you. But I want to use my degree, and until someone builds a library in this village, working at the Prince estate is my best chance. Let me at least give it a try."

Dr. Richter kissed her on the forehead as he rose to go to bed. "I hope it exceeds your expectations in every way."

~

Isabelle's walk to the Prince estate the next morning was entirely different. The presence of the sun utterly transformed the landscape. No longer a slate gray, the sea sparkled like a liquid sapphire. Every blade of grass, freshly scrubbed the day before, seemed to radiate life. Lazy clouds drifted overhead, spilling velvet shadows on the brilliant landscape below, and a soft breeze brought a gentle reminder of the last days of winter.

Isabelle was sorely tempted to skip part way up the path, but she knew there were eyes in the village watching her even now. Her own reputation mattered little, but her actions also reflected on her father.

The little robot Cog met her at the door again, but this time he was accompanied by Mrs. Kettler. The housekeeper seemed a bit flustered today. She was wearing an apron dusted in flour. Several unruly wisps of hair had broken free from her tidy bun and there were traces of flour on her chin, blouse, and hands. But she seemed cheerful enough.

"Thank heavens the sun has come out," Mrs. Kettler said as she showed Isabelle to the library. "One can only stomach so much gloomy weather. Between you and me, it doesn't help the Master any. He pulls all the curtains and sulks in the dark like a bear in hibernation."

Isabelle smiled at the woman's affectionate description.

"Sometimes, when the sun is shining, I can get away with opening the windows and it does him a world of good, though he'd never admit it."

Mrs. Kettler swung open two heavy wooden doors and led Isabelle into the library. It was so dark that at first they couldn't see anything. The housekeeper flipped the switch for the lights, but nothing happened. She made a noise of disapproval with her tongue.

"It's been so long since anyone's been in here, the lightbulbs must have blown. I'll see that Luis replaces them by tomorrow." Mrs. Kettler navigated across the floor and pulled the drawstring just beside the vaulted windows. Both curtains slid into motion at once, letting in a flood of sunlight and sending the dust motes swirling.

"Luis?" Isabelle asked as she surveyed the grand room absentmindedly.

"Our footman, of sorts." Mrs. Kettler returned to her side. "I suppose you might call him a handyman. Now, do you need anything else, dear? I really ought to get back to the kitchen."

"No. Thank you! I have what I need."

After another smile, Mrs. Kettler bustled away, leaving Isabelle to thoroughly examine the library in peace.

Great empty shelves stretched from the floor to the vaulted ceiling, twenty feet overhead, broken up by an elegant catwalk that ran the length of the wall in between the two sets of floor-to-ceiling windows. Behind her and to her left an ornate carpet had been stretched before a great fireplace, and furnished with a settee and two comfortable sofas. The rest of the floor was completely covered in unopened boxes.

Only the far right wall had been partially shelved, and a quick inspection of the occupants proved them to be old textbooks and outdated scientific journals. Isabelle felt a sudden twinge of alarm and threatening disappointment. Was that all these boxes were filled with? Stodgy academic work? She pried open the lid on one of the boxes. The friendly faces of Dickens, Melville, and Tolstoy sent a familiar thrill down her spine.

"Right then." She turned to Cog, who blinked his large turquoise eyes at her in eager anticipation. "We need to see what we're working with. You are a very fetching robot, but they don't keep you around just for your looks, do they?"

Cog shook his head.

"Do you have a Bluetooth connection in that little head of yours?"

The robot nodded.

Isabelle pulled a tablet out of her satchel and held it out to him. He took it reverently, then virtually connected the device to his CPU with a series of nimble keystrokes. He handed it back to Isabelle and swung his arms gleefully.

Isabelle smiled at him. "Shall we begin the inventory?"

Cog scurried to the farthest box, deftly broke the seal, and began scanning barcodes. Isabelle organized the information as it came in.

For being so small, Cog was remarkably fast. The new books were the easiest, but the pair soon found that this library collection boasted books from every century, in multiple languages, and in varying conditions. The older ones did not have barcodes and some didn't have a cover at all.

By eleven, they had made a thorough mess of the room, but Isabelle had begun to form a solid plan for documentation, categorization, restoration, and further research. Then a message came through from Cog, calling for her evaluation on an entire box. She waded carefully through boxes and piles of books to investigate.

The first thing that caught her eye was a diploma awarded to Sebastian Prince for a PhD in Neuro-Technology. She frowned in surprised confusion before continuing her investigation. Besides the diploma there were also two dissertations in Sebastian's name, an assortment of papers, and an external hard drive.

She pulled them out and set them on a side table, making a mental note to ask Mrs. Kettler about them. But when Isabelle packed up to go, the housekeeper was nowhere to be found.

Isabelle looked down at the stack in her hands and then at Cog. "I don't suppose Mr. Prince has an office?"

Cog wiggled excitedly and took off down the hall. Isabelle followed with a smile. By the time she caught up to him, the door was open for her. What she found when she stepped inside wasn't an office but a laboratory.

Cables hung from the ceiling, giving power to the clusters of equipment that dotted the room like mechanical bushes. In the far left corner she spotted a reclining chair surrounded by monitors. Right beside it sat the closest thing to a desk. It was a workbench covered by an assortment of papers and tablets.

"Excuse me, Mr. Prince?" There was no reply. Isabelle crossed the room and laid her finds on the workbench. Her eyes caught sight of the top of a piece of paper. She picked it up curiously. It appeared to be a contract, dated three years ago. Her eyes skimmed over thick blocks of text that she couldn't understand and landed on a formidable seal at the bottom: Department of Defense.

"Who let you in here?" a powerful voice spoke from just behind her, making her jump.

"I'm sorry, I didn't mean to intrude. I found something in the library—"

Sebastian spotted the paper in her hand and snatched it from her. Isabelle, feeling a bit guilty, struggled to find words. Rage began to kindle in his face when he recognized what she had been holding. The veins in his neck began to bulge again and his hands trembled.

"You have no business reading this." The words came out forcefully, as if he could barely breathe.

Her cheeks turned scarlet. "I'm sure you're right. Please forgive me."

"Forgive you?" he scoffed. His disdain gave her courage.

"My father always said I was too curious for my own good. I didn't mean any harm."

"Who's your father?" he asked sharply.

Her heart faltered for a moment, warning her somehow that he wouldn't like the answer. "Dr. Maurice Richter."

His hand clenched suddenly, crushing the paper in his hand. "You've come to spy on me," he hissed. His chest rose and fell rapidly and his eyes were glazing over.

"No," Isabelle said gently, confused by his anger.

"You've come to sabotage my work—to make me a laughing stock!" He stepped toward her threateningly, his eyes wild and bloodshot.

She took a step backwards and lifted her hands, but her voice remained calm and low. "Mr. Prince, it was wrong for me to enter your lab without permission, and I had no business touching your papers." She gestured decidedly toward the workbench, knowing it would help separate her from the source of his anger. "But I assure you that I meant no harm."

Sebastian looked like he was about to explode. She drew a line in her mind: if he took one more step toward her, she would run. Instead, he reached for the nearest shelving unit and gave it a forceful shove, sending the equipment hurtling to the floor in a cacophony of shrieking metal and splintering glass.

Isabelle stood her ground. It was not lost on her that he had deliberately chosen to take his anger out on an inanimate object instead of her. He may not look in control of his anger, but he was making choices, just as he had the first day she had met him.

"Can you tell me what is making you so angry?" she asked, fighting back tears. "I want to make this right, but I can't read your mind."

He did not seem to hear her. He turned away with a desperate destructive energy that Isabelle had seen once before: throwing monitors, ripping cables free, and shoving scaffolds to the floor.

Isabelle was not afraid anymore. Compassion stirred in her heart for this man who was clearly a victim of his own emotions. By the time his rampage had ended, his shoulders were shaking with emotion and his hands and forearms were cut and bruised. He seemed surprised to find that Isabelle was still there.

"Have you had your share of amusement?" he asked bitterly.

"Why would you think I'd find this amusing?" Isabelle thought her heart might break.

"Why else did you come here?"

"I was looking for work. The villagers sent me up here. I'm pretty sure they expected you to scare me off."

"They think I'm a wild animal," he said.

"I'm sure nobody thinks that."

"No, they do." His voice trembled. "I've heard them say it."

She cleared her throat. "Well, they don't have very nice things to say about me, either. I don't suppose you have a first aid kit around here?"

He gestured to the wall. She crossed the room, opened it, and began pulling out an assortment of items. When she returned, he looked hesitant.

"I can clean myself up." A hint of hardness returned to his eyes.

"I'm sure you can comb your hair, too, but it's clearly not on your list of priorities. Now sit down. If I don't do it, I imagine it will fall to Mrs. Kettler, and she has enough to worry about. Unless you've taught Cog how to administer first aid." Isabelle took a seat on the floor.

At the mention of his name, Cog emerged from the far end of the room and came to stand beside Isabelle, one of his little hands resting on her shoulder. Sebastian conceded and sat across from them. Isabelle donned her gloves and looked at him expectantly. He held out his arm.

"I suppose that explains how you got into the lab." His voice was thick, gravelly, and tired. His eyes were on Cog.

Isabelle touched an alcohol swab to his arm. He tensed up, but didn't withdraw. "I really should stop following him," she said. "He keeps taking me places I'm not supposed to be."

The corner of Sebastian's mouth turned up. "He seems to have developed a liking for you."

"Isn't that how you programmed him? To be generally adorable?" She spread a bandage over a network of small lacerations.

"He has a personality matrix, yes. But his imprinting programming was experimental. He doesn't attach himself to many people." Sebastian's eyes were fixated on her face.

Isabelle felt heat creeping up her neck. "Well, then. I shall consider myself privileged."

Mrs. Kettler stepped through the door. "Oh dear. Not a good day, then, Mr. Prince?"

Sebastian stood quickly.

"Shall I begin ordering new equipment?" the housekeeper asked.

"Get it here quickly. I don't care what it costs." His voice had become tight again.

Mrs. Kettler appeared surprised when her eyes fell on Isabelle. "Miss Richter, I did not know you were still here."

"Just heading out now." Isabelle scrambled to her feet. "I will see you tomorrow morning."

Sebastian kept his eyes averted as she left the lab.

The spring day was at its full glory as Isabelle walked home, but this time it failed to draw a smile from her. Her brows were drawn and her eyes limited themselves to the path in front of her feet as her mind replayed the scenes from the morning.

As she approached the village, her reverie was broken by the chatter of friendly voices. She took a deep breath and returned to the present, trying to remember if she had tomatoes to use for dinner.

"Good afternoon, there!" an old man called.

Isabelle smiled. "Afternoon!"

"You lost me a ten-er."

"I beg your pardon?"

"I bet me neighbor the beast would chew ya up and spit ya out!" The man laughed.

Isabelle crossed her arms. "That's a strange way to talk about one of your foremost families."

"Is that what our Grocer told you?" The man chuckled again. "He was just trying to pull one over on you."

"Why do the people in this village seem to take great amusement in being cruel?" Her temper was growing short.

"I suppose it was a little unjust to send you up there with no warning," the man admitted.

"Sebastian Prince is not a monster," Isabelle said firmly. A fire had lit in her and the heat was creeping up her face.

"You know that for sure, do ya? After being here a few days? There's something sure not right with him."

"Should that not evoke compassion instead of disdain?" It took a great deal to keep from yelling.

"Oh, you won't find compassion for that man in this village."

"Why not?"

"I don't pretend to understand what draws these scientists to come here, something to do with magnets."

"Magnetic anomalies," Isabelle corrected automatically. She had heard her father speak about it often enough.

"Well, we didn't ask for it," the man said petulantly. "When he came five years ago, he was like all the others: promising that his scientific advancements would be good for the village, but all they brought was harm."

"What harm?"

"It ain't right to mess with the mind."

"Surely, he didn't experiment on the villagers." She held her breath for a moment.

"Not with our permission. But people started having strange dreams. And then one day Mrs. Lewis' boy didn't wake up. He slept for two days straight then started screaming bloody murder, but still he wouldn't wake up. He died two weeks later!"

Isabelle's anger dissipated slightly and her voice dropped. "That's terrible. But why would you think Mr. Prince had anything to do with it?"

"Cause he owned up to it! He came down when he heard the boy was in a coma and he told the mother that he was gonna make it right. But nothing was made right! That's when they say he lost his mind. Most folk say it was justice long overdue."

Isabelle's eyes wandered up the hill. "If that's justice," she whispered, "I don't particularly like it."

"Well, that sentence don't come from no earthly judge. Excuse me, the missus is calling." The man scurried back to his house, leaving Isabelle to her thoughts. She hardly saw the cobblestones beneath her feet as she walked the rest of the way to her house. Her mind was tossing like a stormy sea.

She did not find tomatoes at home, but she made do without them, dreading a trip to the Grocer's. Her mind was heavy as she set the house in order and washed the laundry. She put together a simple casserole and popped it into the oven, then sat down with a book to wait for her father. There was no wind or rain that night, and the silence that descended on the cottage with the dark made her feel incredibly lonely.

She started when the doorknob turned, but was relieved to set about the final preparations for dinner. Dr. Richter noticed the care in his daughter's face, but he did not ask about it until after the meal was eaten, the dishes were washed, and he had exhausted conversation on his own work.

"How was your day with the mysterious Sebastian Prince?" He asked.

"Not what I expected," she said, weighing her words carefully. "He has a doctorate in Neuro-Technology."

Dr. Richter's eyebrows shot up in surprise. "Well, that explains why the villagers don't like him. But why is he anathema to the scientific community?"

"I'm not sure I have all the details, but it sounded like he took responsibility for a tragic death in the village."

Dr. Richter exhaled deeply in understanding. "Thus, he became the pariah of both communities."

"It's a bit more than I reckoned for in a day job," she admitted, struggling to keep the emotion out of her voice. She told herself angrily that she had no reason to cry.

Her father was casually swinging his reading glasses between his fingers, but his sharp eyes were on her face. "You plan to continue, then?"

Isabelle did not look at him. Even so, it took her a moment before she could get the words out. "I think I would regret it later if I backed out now. Mr. Prince's struggles really have little to do with the job Mrs. Kettler hired me for."

Her father's silence told her he was unconvinced. Despite her best efforts, a tear slipped down her face. She tried to hide it before he could see, but it was too late. He knelt by her chair and tilted her chin up until her eyes met his.

"There's no need for you to feel unsafe."

"I don't feel unsafe. Maybe I'm a fool, but I don't think he would hurt me."

"I have never thought you a fool," he said. "But I have heard enough to know that being there is bound to bring up painful memories for you."

She wiped away another tear. "I want to help him. The villagers talk about him like he's an animal, and I'm sure that's how they've treated him. They don't understand how much pain he's in. I don't understand it either, but I see it. And I'm in a better position than most people to handle it."

"Isabelle, if this is about you feeling guilty—"

"This is about me turning those years into something good," she said meaningfully. "I think it's what mother would have wanted."

Pain flickered across his face. "I so wanted us to make a fresh start here."

"We will." She smiled at him reassuringly, wiping her watery eyes. "We are going to build a good life here. This is something that I need to do."

~

A northern wind picked up that night, driving in a fine rain. The morning in Maple House did not begin smoothly. Isabelle dropped her father's favorite mug and then burnt her hand pulling scones from the oven. She left the house a few minutes later than she had intended and attempted to make up for it with a quicker pace.

The soggy earth squelched beneath her rain boots as she marched up the lonely path to the great house on the cliff. Her brave words to her father the night before seemed a bit hollow this morning as she considered facing another emotional tempest today. It must be the gloomy weather that had her thinking this way.

She was rather glad when Cog was the only one to meet her at the door. They made their way to the library together and Isabelle's heart was soothed by the familiar routine of the work.

The storm outside grew worse, sending rain pelting against the large, panel windows. But all was peaceful within. The only other sounds besides the driving rain were the opening and closing of books, the rustling of pages, and the pitter patter of Cog's little feet as he scurried about. Today they were to start shelving, and she was eager to see the end result. Cog had already begun on the lower levels. After testing the reliability of the dusty old ladder, Isabelle began working on the higher shelves.

Around mid-morning, she heard the door open and carefully descended the ladder, fully expecting to meet with Mrs. Kettler. But the master of the house himself appeared, balancing a tea tray precariously in his hands. Noticing his bloodshot eyes and how uncomfortable he looked with it, she helped guide it to the coffee table in front of the fireplace.

"Mrs. Kettler thought you might like a cup of tea…and I thought it might be a good opportunity to apologize." He swallowed.

It was strange to see him so unsure of himself.

"How do you like your tea?" she asked.

He hesitated.

"You're not going to make me take my tea alone, are you?" There was a slight reproach in her voice.

"I wasn't sure you'd want me for company," he said.

"Well, we had better do something while we wait for you to apologize." Her eyes twinkled a bit mischievously.

"Cream, no sugar," he replied, taking a seat.

She busied herself with the tea service, occasionally stealing glances at the subdued face of her companion. "I'm naturally curious, Mr. Prince, but I know how to restrain myself if I'm given limits. I think it would be worthwhile for both of us if I were to learn yours."

"Call me Sebastian. I don't deserve any other title. And as for my limits," he smiled ruefully, "I don't even know those." Pain contorted his face and his teacup began to rattle so forcefully that he had to set it on the table. He put his head in his hands and breathed heavily. "I'm sorry."

"What are you apologizing for?" She asked.

"For not even being able to have a decent conversation," he gasped. Frustration was creeping into his voice and body language.

"Keep breathing and let it pass." Isabelle held her teacup steady. "There's no hurry on a stormy day like this."

He did not lift his face from his hands, but after a few moments, his shoulders stopped heaving.

Isabelle sipped her tea calmly. "Have you ever tried to train Cog to carry tea for you? He's just about the perfect height for a walking tea table. I imagine it'd be awfully useful at parties, too."

"How do you do that?" he asked in a husky voice.

"Do what?" she asked.

"Take whatever is thrown at you and reflect something better?"

She set her teacup in her lap and stared at it for a long moment, wrestling with the sudden anxious fluttering in her chest.

"My mother was in a car accident when I was sixteen. She was thrown from the vehicle, and though she didn't die, she suffered a traumatic brain injury." Isabelle took a moment to breathe. "She became a different person—forgetful, stubborn, irritable. Not just irritable," she corrected. "Enraged. I used to think it was my fault."

Isabelle pursed her lips and struggled to continue. "All I wanted was my mother back. I resented her and I felt so guilty for it." She looked up at Sebastian with wet eyes. For the first time since she had met him, his seemed completely clear.

"My father and I did everything we could to learn more about her condition, how to read her moods and calm her down when she was upset."

"What happened?" he asked.

"She died, three years ago. There was a blood clot in her brain."

"I'm sorry," he said.

"I've always wondered, if she had had more time, if she would have eventually come back to us," she said.

"You still had hope for her after all of that?"

"I did," she said. "I think the human brain has a remarkable ability to heal when it's given the right care."

He was staring at the teapot.

Isabelle took a deep breath and gently changed the subject. "Sebastian, I heard about what happened a few years ago with the boy in the village. But what you're struggling with is more than just guilt. Has anyone ever asked what happened to you?"

The flames rekindled behind his eyes. He stood to his feet and spoke through clenched teeth. "It doesn't matter what happened to me."

"It does to me," she protested. "I understand better than you know, and I want to help."

She watched him struggle with himself for a few long moments and was afraid he might leave the room. For once, his rational side seemed to win out.

"I was working on a project for the Department of Defense." He stood facing the window, his back half-turned to her.

"They were interested in my research involving the amygdala and the brain's connection to technology. They wanted me to explore the possibilities of weaponization—neural warfare. Weapons that could cripple the enemy's mind."

He paused. "You have to understand, I was using their funding to advance medical technology and turn the clock back on cognitive disease. My projects for the DOD was just a fraction of my work, and I never thought…"

Isabelle stood beside him, placing a hand on his shoulder. He tensed at first, but then relaxed.

"I was experimenting with shared dreaming through specific frequencies. I was tired. That night there was a surge in this region's electro-magnetic energy and I didn't catch it. It amplified the frequency field and caught the outermost house in the village."

Sebastian spoke a bit more easily now that he'd reached the technical part, as if he had just crested a hill. "It wasn't ready for human testing yet. His brain waves were restricted from their natural cycles. He was caught in the shared dream space, with figments of his own imagination. After dreaming constantly for two days, his cortisol levels rose and flooded his amygdala. In the end, his brain just couldn't take the strain."

He stepped away from her touch and began pacing, clenching and unclenching his hands. "Perhaps it wasn't a good idea to have this conversation." He tried to laugh, but it came out as more of a strangled cry.

Outside the window, lightning flashed over the ocean, soon followed by a rippling crack of thunder.

Isabelle took a deep breath to steady herself. "You went in after him, didn't you?"

Sebastian picked up a book and began thumping it against the wall as he walked.

"I'd rather you didn't damage the books," she said as casually as she could.

"I have to do something," he snapped. His face was completely red now, his movements becoming desperate. "I can't...there's too much...and it's going to come out some way or another!"

He dropped the book and turned to the wall, but she read his intentions and intercepted him before he could throw his first punch.

"No, no, no!" she cried, taking his hands. "You're liable to break a bone or damage my library walls that way. I don't do woodwork, and I don't much like cleaning up blood."

He was gasping for air, every muscle in his body trembling with adrenaline. "I'm not sure you should touch me. I don't want to hurt you," he panted.

Isabelle drew one of his hands to her chest so he could feel her even breathing and placed her other hand on the side of his face. "You're not going to hurt me. Deep breaths. Close your eyes and listen to the sound of the rain. There we go. Just breathe in and out. In a second here, we can have another cup of tea and watch the waves roll in."

Sebastian's breathing calmed significantly and she knew he was past the crisis moment. He pulled away from her and crossed to stand in front of one of the tall windows. She watched his breathing return to normal and the muscles in his shoulders relax, then came and stood beside him.

"There's nothing to be ashamed of."

"I'm a grown man," he hissed angrily, "but I'm trapped in my own mind and body."

"Sebastian, your brain has been wounded. You just need a little more help."

"A little more help?" he spat the words out. "It's been three years. Three years of feeling out of control, like a wild animal."

"The brain has a remarkable ability to heal," she repeated.

"Then wouldn't it have done it by now?" he asked. "Did your mother's brain heal?"

Isabelle put a hand to her mouth.

"I'm sorry, I shouldn't have said that." He hurried out of the room, closing the door forcefully behind him.

∼

Isabelle headed home early that day, leaving a note with Cog for Mrs. Kettler. She stumbled down the hill and through the village, fighting back tears with every step. They broke free as soon as she closed the door behind her.

She curled up on the couch with a thick blanket and allowed herself a good cry, fully intending to set the house in order afterwards. Sleep claimed her first, and it didn't release her until the light was beginning to fade. She woke to the high-pitched shriek of an angry wind and the electronic sound of her phone vibrating.

It was a text message from her father. He would not be home tonight. It seemed to confirm to her that the day was irredeemable. She wearily made herself ready for bed with the hope that tomorrow would be better. But it was a fitful sleep with little rest, and it ended abruptly in another vibration from her phone. But it wasn't her father calling, as she had expected. She frowned as she answered the phone.

"Hello?"

"Isabelle? It's Dr. Glass. I think you'd better come down to the lab."

~

Isabelle flew out the door with wild hair and her coat on backwards. The village was enshrouded in an icy cloud, preventing her from seeing anything beyond three feet. The half-frozen drops of water pricked at her face and neck like tiny swords. Her boots pounded on the cobbled streets with dull, lifeless thuds. The village seemed uncharacteristically quiet, but Isabelle was glad of it. She didn't want to be seen.

The lab rose up cold and forbidding in front of her, like a ghost out of the fog. Isabelle's cold fingers fumbled on the handle, but it opened from the inside and a kindly old man who must be Dr. Glass took Isabelle's arm. He held her still for a moment and looked intently in her eyes.

"What's happened?" she asked breathlessly. "Was there an accident?"

"I'm afraid this may be difficult to explain…but he won't wake up."

A pit settled in Isabelle's stomach. "Let me see him. Now, please."

He led her down a hall into a small room, where she found her father stretched out on a cot. His skin was pale and his breathing shallow, but other than that he appeared to be simply sleeping. She stroked the side of his face gently. "Papà?"

There was no response. She shook him gently, knowing how foolish she must look to Dr. Glass. But he handed her a cup of water, as if understanding that she needed to see for herself. She poured it on her father's face, hoping desperately to see him suck in a startled breath and glare at her. But he did not move.

"I have tried multiple stimuli," Dr. Glass said. "Nothing works. I know this may seem very strange to you, but I have seen this before—"

Isabelle stood suddenly and faced him. "You will watch over him?"

"Where are you going?" Dr. Glass asked in surprise.

She left him without an answer and re-emerged into the gray morning with fiery resolve. The Prince estate was only about a quarter-mile from the lab, and Isabelle's feet nearly kept pace with her pounding heart.

Fear, frustration, anger, and sorrow ebbed and flowed like a fickle storm within her. But as she neared her destination, a surprising sound met her ears: angry voices. Up here on the cliff, the relentless sea breeze had cleared the fog a little and Isabelle spotted a crowd gathered at the foot of the great stairs. It almost looked like the whole village had turned out, and more were coming up the path. Many of them held torches, and their eyes were fixed on two men pounding on the front door of the mansion.

"What's happened?" Isabelle slipped into the crowd.

"That monster's up to his old tricks! Preying on the innocent!" a woman answered.

"This time, there's three that won't wake up!" someone else added.

"This time he's not going to get away with it!"

Isabelle's stomach clenched and she pushed her way through the crowd and up the steps.

A man stepped in front of her. "Where do you think you're going?"

"Please, I've been working at the Prince estate the last few days. Let me find out what's going on."

"We know well enough what's going on." A man came up beside them, holding a rifle. "Let's end this now."

"Are you going to shoot someone?" Isabelle asked in disgust.

"If that's what it takes."

"Is that what passes for justice around here?" She turned to address the whole crowd. "You all take pride in hard work and tradition, and I respect that. But there is no honor in confronting an unarmed man like this. My father won't wake up either. And although Dr. Prince may be responsible, he also may be the only one who can help. Please, let me go in and speak to him!"

"He hates us! What makes you think you can change his mind?"

"Give me fifteen minutes. It can't do any harm."

The crowd appeared hesitant, but the man who had been holding Isabelle back escorted her up the rest of the stairs.

"Fifteen minutes," he said gruffly. "Then we'll do what needs doing."

Isabelle swallowed, then pounded on the door with trembling hands. "Mrs. Kettler, please let me in! It's Isabelle!" She hoped she didn't sound as desperate as she felt.

The door cracked open, and Isabelle slipped through as fast as she could before slamming it shut behind her and bolting it. The pressure in her heart eased up a bit until she saw the faithful housekeeper's face. Mrs. Kettler appeared to have aged ten years. Her chin was set firmly, but there was fear in her eyes.

"You shouldn't have come," she said to Isabelle. "They're liable to kill you along with the rest of us."

"Where's Dr. Prince?"

"He can't give them what they want."

"Please let me speak with him."

"He can't speak with anyone," Mrs. Kettler said wearily. "He's hooked up to that cursed machine again, and I fear this time it'll kill him."

"He's in the shared dream space?" Isabelle asked.

"He did not tell you everything." Mrs. Kettler beckoned for Isabelle to walk beside her. "He told you he went in to try and save that boy?"

"Yes."

"Did he tell you how he woke up?"

Isabelle hesitated. Why had she never thought of that before?

"The concept of the shared dream space had been around for years, but nobody could get it to work. It was Master Prince who postulated that it needed to source from a human amygdala, not just a machine. He was not approved to use test subjects, so he tested it on himself."

"Is that when the boy got pulled in?" Isabelle asked.

"Yes, but you are not listening to me. His brain is linked to that machine. The nightmares and terrors in that dream space are his, and they grow every day in strength. The machine is attached to his mind. He cannot be free of it, not even while he is awake."

"Why did he not just destroy it?"

"We feared the damage it would do. And he has somehow maintained hope that he could make things right."

"But what happened today?"

"He went back in sometime in the night. I found him several hours ago. But this time I cannot wake him."

They had arrived at the lab. Sebastian was lying in the reclining chair that Isabelle had spotted two days before. The monitors around him were singing a cacophonous chorus of bad news: brain waves erratic, pulse too high, blood pressure too high, cortisol levels rising. Even his skin looked unnaturally grey.

Isabelle swallowed. How much time had passed since she'd entered the house?

A small hand touched her leg. Cog looked up at her with those large turquoise eyes. She stooped down in front of him.

"Cog, have you been helping Dr. Prince with this machine?"

Cog nodded.

"How do we shut it down once and for all?"

Cog pattered over to a shelving unit, removed a tablet, and handed it to Isabelle. He pointed to his antenna as words appeared on the screen: *Dr. Prince must shut it down from inside.*

"Can I help him?"

Cog nodded. One of his tiny metallic hands touched her face and then a scanner activated in his eyes. A second later a brain scan appeared on the tablet. Cog pointed to it eagerly.

Isabelle looked at him in amazement. "Is this why you let me in that day?"

Cog nodded again.

Isabelle stood suddenly and addressed Mrs. Kettler. "Can you get out the back without them seeing you?"

"Do you expect me to leave you and Master Prince?"

"There's no point in you staying." Isabelle put a hand on the housekeeper's arm. "Please get somewhere safe. Maybe you can do some good outside."

Fighting back tears, Mrs. Kettler embraced Isabelle roughly and then retreated out the door. Cog sealed the lab behind her and returned to Isabelle's side.

"Tell me what to do, Cog."

Cog pressed a series of buttons, and a low table slid out from the wall. Discarding her jacket, Isabelle rolled up her sleeve and held it out for Cog who applied an IV and hooked her up to the rest of the medical monitors. She lay back and took deep breaths.

Cog inserted something into her IV and the two metal wires attached to her temples began to vibrate. She felt a sudden shock and then the scene around her changed.

~

She was standing in a dark cavern. A faint light source glinted off damp walls. The sound of dripping water echoed eerily, changing octaves unexpectedly like the notes of a ghostly tune. The tiny feet of invisible insects skittered through the sand and up the cavern walls. Isabelle tried to steady her heartbeat. She couldn't shake the feeling that, whichever direction she moved, she'd run into a web containing a giant spider. And yet, she had not entered this dream space to do nothing. She had to move.

She forced herself forward, shuffling her feet one step at a time. The ground began to slope. Isabelle reached for the left wall instinctively. Her fingers met with a gooey substance. She gasped, but did not withdraw her hand. She pressed forward foot by foot, reminding herself that none of this was real. Then the ground dropped out from beneath her, and she plummeted into a cesspool of putrid liquid.

Something brushed her leg in the water, and she surfaced with a strangled cry, reaching out desperately for any way out of the water. A distant shriek echoed about the cavern. Isabelle's groping fingers found a rock ledge just as something wrapped around her left leg.

She heaved herself up, kicking furiously and trying not to wretch. Her leg came free, and she scrambled farther up the bank before allowing herself to collapse in a trembling heap. The water continued to slosh and churn behind her. She needed to get out of this cave and find Sebastian.

Her heart was pounding so hard it hurt. Every muscle in her body was trembling with adrenaline, and she could taste bile at the back of her mouth, but now she was angry. She got to her feet and forced herself forward, stumbling over gaping shadows, through spider webs, and past chambers with bone-chilling sounds coming out of them. None of it would deter her. After what seemed like an eternity, she burst out into the open night air and gasped in relief. The mouth of the cave grew larger behind her, as if trying to suck her back inside. She stumbled forward into the woods.

The forest would hold its own dangers, but Isabelle allowed a false sense of relief to wash over her. Her body needed a break. She pressed forward blindly for a few minutes, breathing slowly and not dwelling on the shadows around her. But seeking out safety was not her priority. She had to find Sebastian. How was she supposed to do that in this wild place? Her eyes caught sight of a series of ghostly spires rising above the forest. A fearsome red light pulsed from one of the highest rooms, and Isabelle knew immediately that this was her destination.

Almost as soon as she altered her course, she heard the first wild howl. She pressed forward, scrambling over fallen logs that teemed with hissing insects. Large sets of orange eyes glared at her from the underbrush. Her hands were covered with dirt and moss. The wolf cries seemed to be getting closer.

Large white flakes began to drift down from the canopy, and within a few minutes, a steady snow had begun to fall. She started to slip more frequently, catching herself on raw palms, which had turned red from cold. She was nearly to the outer wall of the castle when she heard the sound of padded steps in the undergrowth around her. She caught sight of shadows darting on her left and right, sometimes high in the trees.

She came up against a tangle of thorns and briars too thick for her to pass through and turned to her right. A dark shadow hunched ten feet away from her, dark as night with gleaming yellow eyes, and a square jaw the size of her head. Its shoulders twitched as if preparing to pounce.

Isabelle turned and fled, knowing it was hopeless. That monster would be upon her in seconds, tearing her to pieces with its sharp teeth. Even now it seemed to have its claws in her heart, squeezing so tight she thought it would explode from the pressure. She caught sight of it in the tree to her right just before it pounced.

The giant panther knocked her to the ground and they both tumbled down a slight incline. Its breath on her face and the heat of its body seemed to be the very embrace of death itself. A claw sliced her left arm.

She struggled to hold back its mighty head with her small hands.

Suddenly, the panther was ripped off her by a great and terrible force. She struggled to sit up, leaves and twigs pulling at her hair. Two large shadows wrestled in the darkness, yelping and growling as they tumbled back and forth.

Isabelle did not stay to watch. She scrambled away on her hands and knees, ignoring the thorns and rocks that tore at her skin. After about twenty feet she made it to her feet and resumed her headlong plunge into the foliage. Her chest ached and her heart burned with fear.

Something tried to surface in her mind—something she needed to remember. This wasn't real; it was a dream. She needed to find Sebastian. A great shadow, the size of a boulder leapt in front of her, then stretched to its full height, nearly twelve feet tall. The massive bear opened its maw and gave a roar that shook the ground, reducing Isabelle's heart to a puddle.

But something else, nearly as large leapt between her and the bear, releasing its own earth-shuddering howl. The bear took a step backwards. The creature in front of her stood its ground and howled again, its voice echoing across the tree tops. The bear dropped on all fours and retreated slowly into the shadows.

Isabelle stood frozen in shock. The dark shadow turned towards her. "What are you doing here?"

She gasped when she recognized Sebastian's voice. He took a step closer to her and threw his cloak about her just as the moon pierced through the clouds, allowing her to see him for the first time.

He towered over her, at least eight feet tall, with arms and legs like tree branches. His eyes were familiar, but the rest of his face was warped and disfigured.

"You shouldn't be in here," he said.

"My father…" She couldn't seem to finish the sentence, but his eyes registered understanding. They filled with regret, and he turned away in shame.

"Sebastian," she said. "There are three this time, and the villagers are terrified. I'm afraid they'll do something rash; they may have already. We need to shut this thing down."

"Don't you think I've tried?" he growled. "The failsafe won't work."

"Show me," she said.

He did not move.

"I did not come in here to let my father die. Show me!"

He led her around the corner of the wall and through a massive gate. As they crossed the courtyard, a wolf chorus rose from the south and was met by an answering chorus from the north. A shiver ran down

Isabelle's spine. Sebastian marched confidently up the stairs and through the main doorway. He snatched up a torch from the wall and proceeded down a series of corridors until they came to a set of stairs.

They wound up and up for several stories until they came out in a small room. In the center, above a pedestal, stood the source of the red light that Isabelle had seen earlier. A very ordinary vase held a single red rose. Red light pulsed from the rose every two seconds. Isabelle looked at Sebastian in amazement.

"Roses were my mother's favorite flower," he said. "I put this one in as a failsafe emergency shut down. Only, I can never seem to touch it."

"How did you wake up last time?" She asked.

"Waking up's not the problem—not for me anyway. I can wake up when I want, but the dream space continues for all of those trapped in it. And somehow…it stays connected to my mind. Sometimes I think I can hear the wolves howling when I am wide awake."

Isabelle approached the rose.

"Be careful," he said.

She reached a hand out gingerly, but an invisible barrier stopped her hand. She turned back to him. There was defeat in his eyes.

"I am so sorry, Isabelle. I never meant for this to happen."

"Of course, you didn't," she said.

"No, you don't understand. I shouldn't have gone back in. I knew what the risks were. I knew others could get trapped in here again."

"Then why did you come back in?" she asked.

"Because I want to live a normal life," he said. "It has been a long time since anyone has seen me the way that you do. And I would give anything for you to see me as the man I used to be."

Tears were forming in Isabelle's eyes.

"And now I've sentenced you and your father to die because of my own selfishness."

The wild howls grew closer and more numerous. A gust blew through the castle, carrying with it a rotten stench. Stories below them, scraping footsteps sounded on the staircase. A wild fear lit in Sebastian's eyes.

"There is one solution that I have not yet tried," he said. "If this dream scape is irrevocably linked to me, then if I cease to exist, it should dissolve."

Isabelle frowned at him. "What are you talking about?"

"I have never died in here." He strode to one of the windows and peered out.

Isabelle came up beside him and took his arm. "Don't be ridiculous. You are not going to kill yourself."

Far below them, the scraping steps grew closer.

"There are things in here far worse than wild animals," he whispered. "I will not let you die because of me. Perhaps this was meant to be all along."

She took hold of his collar firmly. "I have not given up. Whatever is coming, we will face it together."

"It will kill you. Don't do this to me," he pleaded. "Don't make me watch you die."

It struck her as odd that even in this formidable form he was so very vulnerable. He might look like a great big beast in here, but it did not keep him safe from his fears.

"Sebastian," she asked, "have you always taken this form in the dream scape?"

"Not at the beginning, when I was alone," he said. "But as soon as that boy got trapped here, everything became ten times worse and I had to adapt to protect him."

"Do you trust me?" she asked.

"There is nothing we can do," he said hopelessly.

"That is a lie. I know what we have to do. You have to trust me."

His frightened eyes studied her face as the sound of the scraping footsteps drew ever nearer. Then he nodded. "I trust you."

"I know you feel like this is all your fault and that you have to be this big, strong creature to make things right. But you can't hide from your fear, you have to face it. And you have to confront it out of a place of vulnerability."

He looked at her in confusion.

"Drop the mask. I think there is one thing you fear more than that creature coming up the stairs, and it is your own weakness and frailty. The Sebastian that I know is weak, but he is also enough. Stop trying to cover up your weakness. Embrace it."

As she spoke, he began to shrink back to his normal stature. The scars and deformities vanished until he stood before her as a man again. The footsteps on the stairs were growing very loud now, and Isabelle tried not to imagine what it could be that terrified this man so much. He did not turn toward it but approached the rose on the pedestal.

A wave of fear shot out from the rose, sending Isabelle into a trembling heap against the wall. But Sebastian stood strong. He approached the pedestal one foot at a time, fighting against a tide of powerful emotions. Just as Isabelle was certain that whatever horror was on the steps would emerge into the room, Sebastian's hand reached the rose and everything went black.

~

Nothing made sense as Isabelle regained consciousness. She was lying on something soft. There was a bright light overhead and the murmuring of soft voices. The white ceiling above her was such a sharp contrast to the darkness of the dream scape that she lay in shock for a few moments. She stirred under the clean sheets and a figure rushed to her side.

"Papà!"

His strong arms encircled her and pulled her close. His whiskers tickled her cheek and she breathed in the scent of sweat and aftershave, a scent she had thought she would never smell again. He kissed her hair, and when she drew back, there were tears on his cheeks.

"Are you all right?" She took his face in her hands. "When did you wake up?"

"Hours ago. I've been so worried about you."

"What happened?" she asked.

"I don't know how you did it, but you managed to shut that thing off."

"Sebastian!" Isabelle gasped.

Her father's eyes flickered.

"Where's Sebastian? Is he all right?"

"The mob—" he stuttered, "when they did not hear from you after fifteen minutes…they stormed the house."

"What happened?"

"They tossed the furniture through the windows and set the place on fire. You must have stumbled out on your own. We found you unconscious on the grass. I'm afraid Dr. Prince didn't make it out."

"What do you mean?" She clutched the quilt in her fist and tried to keep her voice from trembling. "He's the one who got me out of the dream scape."

"They found his watch and other evidence that he died in the fire."

Isabelle pushed back the blue and white quilt, stood, and made her way to the window. They were very close to the beach, here in the village clinic. Fifty feet away, she could see the surf pounding up on the shore, as predictable as a metronome. Gulls called back and forth as they surfed the heavy wind gusts.

"Mrs. Kettler?" Isabelle asked.

"She's safe."

"Cog?"

"Who?" her father asked.

A great emptiness welled up inside her. "A little robot with the sweetest eyes you've ever seen," she whispered.

"You must mean this little guy," her father replied unexpectedly.

Isabelle whipped around just as her father stooped out the door and picked something up. He returned with Cog in his arms. Isabelle's tears flowed freely as she scooped him up.

"He wouldn't leave your side. He kicked me in the shin when the doctor ordered me to put him out," her father laughed.

"Can we go home now?" Isabelle asked quietly.

~

There wasn't a great deal of talk at Maple House over the next week. Dr. Richter took time off work. Isabelle nearly protested it the first night, not wanting him to worry about her. But all objections left the next day, and she never thought of it again.

They settled into a comfortable routine, taking a long tea in the morning, then reading in companionable silence by the fire. They often went out walking in the afternoons, between rain showers, and Isabelle found her soul soothed by the beauty of the coast. The first afternoon, she insisted on walking up to see the ruins of the Prince estate and say her farewells. Her father offered to come with her, but she insisted she go alone. Despite his fears for her, she returned with a new peace in her eyes.

Cog settled into their home with such efficiency that they soon couldn't remember how they had lived without him. He rose early with Dr. Richter to build the fires, and every night he would retire to his little basket in the living room with a blanket and a book. He would spread his little blanket out and then begin turning pages fastidiously, as he had seen Isabelle do countless times.

Whether or not he understood what he was reading was a subject of great amusement to Isabelle and Dr. Richter. And when Dr. Richter went back to work, it was with the assurance that Isabelle was not alone at home.

Life in the village went on much the same. Most of the villagers didn't want to remember what had happened, and so they acted as if it hadn't. But the one thing everyone seemed able to agree on was that Isabelle was a compassionate, gentle soul, and they began to treat her with kindness.

It was some weeks after the fire that Isabelle was taking tea with Marjorie Williams, a captain's wife.

"You wouldn't mind walking out to the docks with me, would ya dearie?" the woman asked. "Robert's not had anything to eat since before sunrise."

"Of course. What can I carry?"

They packed up their tea and set out for the docks. Marjorie chatted the whole way, and Isabelle, who had often found she did not have much to say these days, was content to listen.

The docks were bustling with friendly activity. A boat had foundered on the rocks two days ago in a nasty storm and now the other fishermen were lending a hand whenever they could to repair it. Marjorie pressed into the noisy throng in bold pursuit of her husband, and Isabelle climbed on a rock to watch, letting the salty breeze toy with her hair.

Her eyes took in the whole scene: the ghostly remains of the Prince estate up on the cliff side to her right, the graceful dance of the birds, the rhythm of the waves, and the frenzied but cheerful activity of the men in front of her. She had learned their names over the last couple of weeks and had even exchanged courteous words with most of them. But as Marjorie returned to her side, Isabelle's eyes fell on the figure of a man who seemed both foreign and familiar.

"Marjorie," Isabelle asked, "who is that man talking to your husband just now?"

"Oh, that's the new one, named Adam."

"He's new?"

"Aye. He came into town a few weeks ago. Not much experience, or conversation, but he's willing enough."

Just then, two of Marjorie's children came running up to show Isabelle the seashell necklaces they had made.

"Where's your brother?" Marjorie asked.

"Up on the rocks." The little girl pointed. "He said he was gonna get a gull's egg for Miss Isabelle."

"He knows he's not allowed up there!" Marjorie exclaimed.

"I'll fetch him," Isabelle offered. "Lucas, come down from there! It isn't safe!" Isabelle picked her way over the tide pools with care. The wind whipped her hair, and spray from the nearby breakers touched her lips.

"Miss Isabelle, I think I could be a bird today!" Lucas extended his arms and looked at the sky wistfully.

"Not today," Isabelle insisted from down below his perch. "You'll frighten your mother. Come have tea with me. I'll give you one of my scones."

The little boy began climbing down obediently, scaling down the rock face directly over the ocean.

"Why don't you come over this way?" Isabelle asked anxiously.

"This way's easier," Lucas insisted. "There's better handholds." But just then, his boots slipped and he plummeted into the surf. Isabelle heard a scream from the beach behind her and jumped in without a second thought.

The surf slammed them up against the rock face, but Isabelle managed to wrap her arms around Lucas and absorb the blow with her body. Salty water sloshed into her mouth and eyes. If they didn't get out of here fast they could get ripped to shreds by the rocks. Lucas wrapped his arms around her, his little body trembling. Isabelle said nothing but held him tight with one arm, trying to gauge the timing of the swells.

They were thrust up against the rocks again and she felt pain shoot through her knee. She shoved off the rocks and began swimming. Her soggy clothes weighed her down, and salt water stung her throat, but she would not give up yet.

They were slammed up against the rocks several more times but managed to stay free from the undertow. Isabelle had never swum so hard in her life.

For several long minutes, she felt certain they were going to drown, but then they rounded the rock outcroppings of the tide pools into open sea.

A crowd had gathered on the shore and two men were wading furiously through the water towards them. Isabelle suddenly found solid ground beneath her feet and dug into it gratefully, holding Lucas tight in her arms. Her water-logged sweater dragged down on her like an anchor. The water was about waist deep when the two men met them. Lucas' father pried the boy from her arms and began scolding him while checking for injury.

Isabelle waved the other man off and kept walking determinedly toward the shore. "I'm fine."

The man stuck close by her side as if he didn't believe her. And when Isabelle stumbled coming up on shore, he caught her arm and lowered her down to the sand.

Her eyes stung, and she began coughing up sea foam that she didn't even know she had swallowed. She vaguely heard him call for water, and her eyes finally settled on his face.

The beard was gone, but she would have recognized those eyes anywhere. The rush of the waves, the cries of the birds, and the hum of the bystanders all faded to the background as Isabelle took a long swig of cool, fresh water, and looked into those eyes she thought she'd never see again. There was something different about them now. They weren't filled with pain and fire, only quietness and peace. She put down the water flask and held out her hand.

"I don't believe we've met."

A genuine smile crossed his face. "I go by Adam."

"Thank you, Adam, for saving my life," she said meaningfully.

His eyes misted over. "Thank you for saving mine."

VOYAGE OF THE PEQUOD

2525
Commonwealth Territory
Massa Colony
New Bedford Space Harbor
The Starship Pequod

◆ ◆ ◆

In the years since the war, New Bedford Space Harbor had gained a paradoxical reputation. It was known to the public as a bit of a 'scabby' place, the unfortunate intersection point for those "less-than-savory" characters who seemed to enjoy shirking society's rules. To anyone who had worked at a Space Harbor, however, it was respected as the most efficient operating harbor in the Commonwealth.

Its population may offend most of the average citizens of the Commonwealth, but its staff and patrons alike had been on the front lines of the war, and they were no strangers to death, loss, and destruction. In the years following the war, they embraced life with the hearty appetite of those always expecting a last meal, yet they continued to run their harbor with military precision and the decisiveness that only comes from dealing with every worst-case-scenario imaginable.

The harbor itself was a striking sight. A dozen jagged asteroids balanced snugly between the gravitational fields of the green planet Bildad and its fiery moon, Peleg. The harbor had been constructed in rings around these jagged asteroids, allowing for a great fleet of ships to dock at once, if need be. New Bedford had rarely been entirely operational, even during wartime. Now almost half of it had been given over to the teeth of time, and only seven docks were maintained on a regular basis. The other five lurked in the background, some still sporting their weapons fire, like monuments to the dead.

The starship *Pequod* was another relic from the war. Its antiquated hull, now patched, had clearly seen better days. It bore only one stripe on its bow, as opposed to the proud three and four stripes of the other, more technologically-advanced ships. Still, its unusual pointed nose and shark-like figure left a remarkable impression next to the newer, geometric vessels docked alongside it. There was an experienced, aggressive aura about it, that whispered of the past. No enemy had conquered it in battle, but neither had it emerged unscathed. The same could be said about its captain.

Yesterday, the *Pequod* had been watered and stocked by its crew under the careful supervision of the first mate. According to the New Bedford Logs, it had been scheduled to depart at 1000 this morning. However, it was now going on 1300 and still it sat at dock. The rest of the New Bedford Space Harbor seemed alive with activity, but the captain of the *Pequod* had not arrived yet, and a ship did not leave without its captain.

Deep inside the forecastle of the *Pequod*, eight men and a boy with the first hints of a beard were seated around a table at the permission of the second mate. The exterior of the *Pequod* may not be much to look at, but the interior was as comfortable as an old rocking chair. Though there was nothing soft about it, over the years it had molded to the shape of its crew, and if you had asked them out of earshot of their wives, they would have called it 'right snug.'

Even to the unacquainted eye it bore certain signs of warmth and affection, whether it was the nicknames painted above the guns, the strange mobile of broken parts that hung in the galley, or the crooked murals that had been drawn by little hands, sent through the mail, and plastered above bunks like fine art. The voyage may not have begun yet, but some of these men had already been gone from home for weeks.

Now this clump of nine sat around the table swapping stories to try and distract themselves from the jitters of impending departure. Nor could they resist an opportunity to have a little fun at the expense of their new shipmate. One of the oldest veterans in particular had been inflating the adjectives in his stories until a newborn would have known better. It greatly amused his shipmates and it made the lad begin to feel wise for catching on. An uproar sounded when the boy addressed the old shipman by the wrong name.

"His name's Ishmael," a voice chimed in quickly. "I'll help you out, lad, before he goes and tells you something different." Laughter erupted from the men around the table.

"Aye, tis a strange name—given by a saucy woman who likely read that Great Book backwards!" Ishmael addressed the boy. "But I think you'll find that I'm not the only one with a spiritual name on this voyage. And that great man," he put a knuckle to his forehead to indicate he was referencing the captain, "was also christened after one of the darker characters—though I won't call his mother saucy." This elicited more chuckles from his companions. "But it just goes to show that even the darker shades of humanity are preferable to the Machines."

"Have you caught any MICs yourself, Mr. Ishmael?"

"Nay, lad. I'm not a harpooner. I just pilot the boat."

"But you've been there when they catch 'em?"

"Aye." Ishmael pulled up the voluminous material of his tunic so his belt was visible. The leather had been punctured with shards of metal, like so many crooked teeth in the mouth of a robotic monster. "I can rightly claim a hand in thirty-two kills."

"They say each MIC shudders and wails when it's captured—almost as if it were really dyin'," the boy whispered anxiously.

"They struggle, all right. They were programmed for self-preservation. But once we get a lance in the motherboard the system is flooded with E.M. liquid. It screws with the motor circuits and frequencies. That's all 'tis. The Enemy's no more alive than your toaster. That's the difference between us and them."

"I think the Captain would disagree with you on that one," another man joined soberly.

"What do you mean?" the boy asked eagerly.

Ishmael dropped his voice to a gravelly whisper. "Well, there's a tale about Captain Ahab, ya see. No one really knows if it's true. It must have been five years ago. He'd just been made Captain of his own vessel and ya never saw a man better suited for the position." Ishmael leaned forward on his elbows. Every man around the table did likewise.

"Everyone knows there ain't no noise in the vacuum of space, right? Well, some folk say that the universe is talking all around us, but it just won't say nothin' to those who won't listen. We humans got five senses, right? And we live our lives and make our decisions by what we take in with 'em, right? Well, once in a while you'll meet someone who's pickin' up another frequency. And their decisions won't make no sense until you realize they got other senses. You get my meanin,' boy?"

"Kinda."

"Captain Ahab's one of those."

"You saying he's a kook?"

"He ain't no kook, boy." Ishmael's voice was even but he slammed a hand on the table, making the boy jump. "He joined the war when he was seventeen—lied about his age. Three years later he was given a battlefield commission and made first lieutenant. But his captain died soon after."

The men had all fallen silent. Business on the dock continued as usual, but it couldn't be heard through the hull. The *Pequod* was tied fast, and yet it seemed to sway ever so slightly as Ishmael continued his story.

"They were out on the fringe and troops were spread thin, so they banded together with whatever ships they could. He ended up commanding a fleet of fifteen—he was the highest ranking officer any of 'em had. And when he weren't around they all called him the Admiral. But of course none of that mattered to the Brass, who didn't see the profit to them in promoting him to do the job he was already doing when it would cost them a bigger paycheck."

The *Pequod* creaked and groaned ever so slightly. The boy licked his lips.

"So he stayed lieutenant for five years. And finally, two years after the war is over they give him his own ship and the rank of Captain. He don't care. He knows his job and he does it. But folks say the only reason they give it to him is because they wanna make a hero out of him. Out of the entire Commonwealth fleet you know how many Captains survived the war?"

The boy shook his head.

Ishmael held up four fingers. "Four. One killed himself two days after the surrender because he'd seen three different crews die before his eyes and he was the only one to survive, only he didn't want to survive no more.

"Two more were completely chopped up, they're gonna spend the rest of their lives in bed. The last one went looney and they shut him up somewhere. So the war's over, but the Commonwealth's facing a decade of patching up the human race and hunting down straggler MICs. But they got no functioning captains. That's when they finally promote him, along with about a dozen other greens who don't know what they're about."

The boy leaned forward with large eyes, fully engrossed in Ishmael's tale. The men around him may have given off a pretense of being bored with the familiar story, but no one interrupted or moved away, and Ishmael seemed well aware that he had a captive audience of more than one.

"But Captain Ahab's their poster boy war hero," the grizzled shipman continued. "Only he don't want to be. They try to take him to parties and parades and show him off to the people, but he don't talk. He's always staring at the walls and asking if his crew can be assigned to the outer limits to hunt down Strags. So finally they lets him. He's seen too much in the war, and he may be no good in the capital, but he's still the soundest captain the fleet ever saw."

Admiration was beginning to glimmer in the boy's eyes.

The pace of Ishmael's storytelling was beginning to pick up. "The ships on the outer edge had been having a dickens of a time killing those straggler MICs. You won't catch me talking nice about any devil Machine. I seen 'em rip apart too many friends. But they are crafty, and you can't deny it. Sometimes they even flock together around a smaller one, as if they're trying to protect it, but I suspect that's calculated like everything else they do.

"They know humans like to read their own behavior into everything else in the universe. Anyhow, when Captain Ahab gets out to the limits, he starts slaughtering 'em. That man can track a MIC through void space better than any bloodhound from old Earth. It's that *other* sense I told you about." Ishmael tapped his temple, knowingly.

"After about six years Captain Ahab and his crew start hearing rumors about this MIC—white as a ghost they say. Big as a ship. And it's mean, they say. Most of the MICs just try to run, ya know. This one picks fights. It shows up out of nowhere when they're about to go for the kill on a littler one. The white ghost shows up and obliterates the ship with a mad vengeance." Ishmael clenched his fist for emphasis.

"Well, they start hearing these stories and Captain Ahab starts thinking he'd better go after it. The estimated kill count of this MIC is close approaching fifty. Only, his best friend and first mate Starbuck says they ought to gather a fleet first; they need to alert the Brass to what's going on and ask for more support. Ahab's fed up with the Brass and he's got no faith in 'em. And the last sightings of this devil ghost indicate he's getting closer and closer to our mining settlements. So Ahab goes against Starbuck and decides to pursue the devil alone."

"What happened?" The boy attempted to keep his tone even, but impatience shone through.

"They found the beast, all right. Put up a good fight. Captain was smart about tactics and he used his boats well. Their ship was nearly smashed to ribbons, but they did real damage, even got a harpoon in its hull.

And it shuddered and stopped moving—as if the E.M. juice had fried it through. Three crewmen are dead, the hull's barely holding together, and Ahab's mad. He wants to go dismember the circuits himself. And Starbuck goes with 'im.

"So they're in their suits floating across to the beast (him, Starbuck, and three others), when it powers up again. It kills the three other men. It nearly killed Starbuck but Captain got in between 'em. It rammed him straight into his own ship and used its own broken hull to sever his leg, almost like a beast hungry for meat. Luckily, his crew acted fast and got him back on board. The MIC hightailed it, and so did they. But they say Ahab lost more than his leg that day, 'cause he ain't never been the same. Some say he'll hunt that white MIC 'til the day he dies."

"But how did it power up again if they'd hit it with a harpoon?" The boy asked.

"No one knows. Some say it was just pretending to be dead."

"Can MICs do that?"

"Of course not, boy. It's just a story!" another man chimed in with a laugh. "There ain't no such MIC."

"Then how did the Captain lose his leg?"

"An engineering accident," someone said.

"Is it true, Ishmael?"

Ishmael did not answer, but he gave the boy a thoughtful look. Just then the bells rang and the call they had all been waiting for sounded: "Captain on deck! All hands!"

The crew responded in smart order, lining up in two neat rows amidships where the Captain and his mates could inspect them from the quarterdeck which overlooked them from the stern. The ship fell silent again and each man kept his eyes directly in front of him until a quiet, commanding voice addressed the first mate.

"Everything appears to be in order, Starbuck. Cast off."

Stations were called and the officers stepped forward, shouting orders to get the vessel underway. Only then did the boy catch sight of his captain. It was just a glimpse, for he wouldn't risk being charged derelict of his duties before they were even out of harbor. But on his way to the second port stabilizer his eyes flitted up to the quarter deck and landed on the man with the Captain's epaulet. Ahab stood sideways now, gazing out the port window at the harbor they were soon to leave behind. He had dark hair, the shadow of a beard, and piercing eyes the color of a glacier. A striking white scar split the left side of his face and disappeared into his collar.

Suddenly his eyes met the boy's. They did not frown in disapproval or widen in surprise. They remained ever-unchanging, still engrossed in the thoughts of the previous moment, as if the course of those thoughts had been charted before by an iron will and nothing from the present reality could alter that course. If those eyes hadn't looked away, the boy may indeed have been derelict in his duties, for he found himself ensnared. But Ahab's eyes returned to the window as if they had never left, and the boy, feeling as if he had just been released from an inexplicable increase in gravity, stumbled to his station wondering how much he might resemble an ant in the captain's eyes, or if he were completely invisible.

Ahab had, in fact, immediately recognized the youngest member of his crew. He always reviewed the files of new crew members extensively. David Pippin had been the subject of great debate between Ahab and his first mate Starbuck. Starbuck had been against the boy coming.

"He's too young," the first mate had said.

"I enlisted at his age," Ahab had replied.

"Well, not everyone's you," Starbuck had answered drily.

Ahab had made no reply. But the next day he had made a quiet investigation into David's references. He had returned with no explanation and a steely resolve to take David on their crew, and Starbuck had trusted his captain's judgment and relented.

But David Pippin was not on Ahab's mind today. His capable mind was delving into deep waters from his past, stirred up by the imminent embarkation of the *Pequod* and thoughts of the journey that lay in store. His officers could handle the details of the launch.

Starbuck, Stubb, and Flask continued to shout their orders and crewmen scurried about to fulfill them. Presently, the effects of those orders became noticeable. The *Pequod* rumbled to life beneath their feet in a series of choppy vibrations that eventually turned to a hypnotic hum. A velvety female voice with a thick accent broadcasted their clearance to depart along a series of specific coordinates. Docking clamps and stabilizers were released and the *Pequod* set sail.

Bildad and Peleg were behind them now, hanging like green and red marbles in the nebulous blue cloud that enveloped the entire colony of Massa. The ringed asteroids of New Bedford Harbor began to shrink, like the cliffs of a distant shore. Before it was out of sight, Ahab had left the quarter deck and disappeared into his cabin. Only Starbuck noticed. The rest of the crew's attention was on what lay ahead.

Ishmael's sharp eyes scanned the deck until they landed on David. Then he looked questioningly at Starbuck, who nodded in understanding. Ishmael crossed the deck and managed to sidle up beside the boy.

"This may sound funny coming from an old codger like me, but I want ye to keep breathing."

"What?" David asked. His eyes were transfixed out the port window above his station, where the blue nebulous cloud seemed to be fading.

"The first time into void space is a right shock, no matter how old ye are."

"I can take it," David muttered. "I've been waiting for this a long time."

"We're going to be traveling at FTL, lad. You ain't never been at those speeds within the colony."

David looked questioningly at the older man.

Ishmael held out a tablet. "Doctor's orders." After another moment's hesitation, David popped it in his mouth. "There's a good lad."

They both turned to watch out the window again. The blue disappeared suddenly, like a vanishing vapor, giving way to the soul-aching black of void space. David had grown up in the blue skies of the Massa colony. They turned a darker hue at night, but they never disappeared altogether. He had only ever experienced total, inky blackness twice in his life and those had both been in confined spaces. Even though the distant glimmer of stars broke up the black canvas, he was still haunted by the knowledge that this darkness encompassed them and extended for trillions of miles.

A soothing voice came over the address system. "All hands prepare for FTL jump in ten, nine, eight…"

As the countdown continued, David felt suddenly certain that he was about to plunge into death itself. Panic gripped his stomach, and he clenched his fists in an effort not to show the fear on his face. A high-pitched whistling had been slowly growing in the background. As the overhead voice reached "one," the whistling crescendoed to a shriek and the darkness in front of them was split asunder by a scalding burst of white light. Distorted shapes and clashes of color streaked past the windows with dizzying speed, and David began to sway.

"Steady there," Ishmael said. But the boy didn't seem to hear him.

Then ten seconds later, the chaos stopped as suddenly as it had begun, and the windows of the *Pequod* were filled with a vibrant collage of rich purple, tangy pink, and milky turquoise. They billowed up in graceful swirls to fearsome heights, interspersed with the pink and orange sparks of various stars. It was a fearsome sight to behold under any circumstances, but physically impossible for most men to process after their first trip through FTL and David promptly passed out.

When he came to, he was lying prostrate on the deck encircled by his amused shipmates. The man who crouched in front of him was the first mate himself, Starbuck.

"You all right, lad?" Starbuck asked.

"What happened?" David's words were a bit slurred.

"You gave into human nature," Starbuck smiled gently, "as each one of us has done before you. It's nothing to be ashamed of."

"But Ishmael gave me some tablet or something," David protested.

"Does your head feel like it's about to split open?" Starbuck asked.

"No."

"That's what the tablet was for." The corner of Starbuck's mouth turned up.

David rolled his eyes, but the men around him chuckled.

"Come on, up you get." Starbuck extended his hand and pulled the boy to his feet. "Welcome to Carina. I'll excuse the lack of proper address, considering the circumstances." Starbuck's voice was gentle and firm. "But don't forget it again."

David's knuckle flew to his forehead. "Yes, sir. No, sir."

"Good. You stick with Ishmael, here. He's a salty old badger, but he'll look out for you."

"Yes, sir."

Starbuck crossed the deck and climbed lithely up the officers' ladder to the quarter deck. His movements bore the same remarkable quality as his voice: gentle, yet firm. He was a tall, slim man who moved with a great deal of grace. Yet there was nothing soft about the first mate. His stern jawline and the toned muscles beneath his uniform spoke of great power under control, and everyone on board respected him, even the most ornery old sailors.

Starbuck was the sort of officer who noticed everything. But his attention to detail, far from provoking resentment and deception, seemed to inspire everyone under him to strive to do better. His only concern on this crew had been the selection of young David Pippin, but he was willing to trust the Captain's judgment and let the boy prove himself. It was the Captain that occupied Starbuck's thoughts now as he rapped lightly on the cabin door at the rear of the quarter deck.

"Enter," Ahab called.

The door slid open with a hydraulic hiss and closed softly behind him as Starbuck stepped in. The captain stood in the center of the room, transfixed by the interactive, holographic display in front of him, his splayed hands manipulating the images and information before him. He did not look up as Starbuck made his report.

"The FTL jump was successful, Captain. We've arrived in Carina and the helmsmen are laying in a course for Genoa, where we're due to rendezvous with Captain Boomer of the Starship *Enderby*." Starbuck did not particularly expect a reply. It was a standard report of information that Ahab already knew. But the contents of the holographic display, combined with the look in Ahab's eyes, drew the first mate's concern. He came up beside his captain.

"Has there been a change in our orders?" Starbuck clasped his hands behind his back. His impeccable posture was a stark contrast to the hunched, tense form of the captain.

"Our orders are to kill MICs," Ahab muttered, not looking over.

"I believe a priority was also placed on protecting the assets and citizens of the Commonwealth," Starbuck replied evenly.

"And do you think that the assets and citizens of the Commonwealth are safe as long as one MIC remains intact?" Ahab asked.

"You want to navigate void space and hunt them down one by one?" Starbuck asked.

"Not one by one. Just one."

"The White MIC hasn't been spotted for fourteen months. It couldn't have survived long after the beating we gave it."

"Oh, it survived," Ahab muttered.

"May I speak freely, Captain?" Starbuck asked respectfully.

"You know you don't need to ask me that question."

Starbuck's muscles relaxed and his clasped hands fell to his sides. "Ahab," he said softly, "you are the most experienced captain in the Commonwealth. The fleet needs your expertise."

Ahab's sharp eyes darted up for the first time. "The White MIC is the greatest threat to the Commonwealth, how can you not see that? You were there!"

"Yes, I was there. I saw it die."

"It came back to life."

"It was a freak, electrical reflex, Ahab. No machine could have re-activated after being hit with the E.M. harpoons."

"That's what I'm saying. This is no ordinary MIC," Ahab said. "Our politicians are hosting parties in the Capital and reports go out documenting unparalleled economic prosperity since the war. Meanwhile our defense outposts lose personnel and funding and slowly decay. Hunting Strags won't even be seen as a viable career for much longer. Even now they tell stories about us as if we were outdated romantics. But what if the war isn't over, Starbuck?"

Starbuck's eyes clouded.

"The Enemy is not a slave to time in the way that we are." A wild light sparked in Ahab's eyes as he grew more animated. "What if they wanted us to think that the war was over, and for the last ten years they have just been biding their time?"

"What advantage could the Enemy have in allowing us time to rebuild?"

"We have rebuilt, but we have also become indolent and lazy."

Starbuck frowned. "It is true that our politicians have come to enjoy the comforts of peace, but I do not think they would have all been so easily deceived."

"Then you have far greater faith in humanity than I."

"If what you believe is true," Starbuck began patiently, "then will we not see signs of it during our tour on the outer edge?"

Ahab shook his head in frustration. "The Council has sent us to Genoa where two other Commonwealth naval ships have been stationed for six months with no action. I begin to wonder if someone on the Council knows of my intention to find the White MIC and wishes to delay us."

"Why would anyone on the Council do such a thing?"

"Because war can bring profit as well as peace," Ahab snapped, "and the heart of man is wicked. Perhaps there is something about the White MIC that someone wants to keep a secret."

"Ahab. Friend. Do you know how this all sounds?" Starbuck asked gently.

The fire in Ahab's eyes was suddenly tempered by great sorrow. "Indeed, I must sound crazy to you. Were I in your position, and my captain told me he had severed all the ship's communications to the Commonwealth and was about to take his crew on a perilous hunt through void space for an unknown duration of time, I might doubt my captain's soundness of mind, and whether he was fit for duty at all." Ahab's tortured eyes were pleading for Starbuck to understand. "But you have always been a better man than I. And I beg of you…if you have ever held me in regard at all, trust me now."

A war raged within Starbuck as he considered his captain. His honor bade him stand by the friend who had saved his life. His good sense reminded him of his responsibility to this crew. And his principals demanded he serve the Commonwealth as an impartial agent. When he finally opened his mouth, he spoke with every fiber of his being.

"I cannot condone the voyage you have planned for us. I fear this will only end badly. But I am with you, Ahab, as I have always been. I know that you would not lead me heedlessly into danger."

Ahab clapped a hand on his friend's shoulder. "I shall endeavor to repay your trust, though it takes a thousand lives and a thousand deaths."

"Nothing so dramatic." Starbuck smirked. "I will follow you through void space, to the edge of the world. Just remember that, at the end of it all, the place I should most like to follow you is back home, to family."

Ahab's eyes glazed over for a moment and doubt flickered on his face. It vanished like smoke, replaced by a steely resolve and black fire in his eyes. He strode from the cabin with the ferocity of a lion.

"Captain on deck!"

The men ceased their work and lined up on the deck below him in expectation. He savored the moment, his eyes passing over his men's faces. Each felt the weight of that glance. It carried with it the driving passion of their captain, like an overwhelming melody that drove their hearts to beat as one. Anticipation rose.

"I know you all signed on for a two year voyage defending the outlying planets of the Commonwealth by hunting down Strags." Ahab's voice was hypnotically soft, but his eyes were loud.

"This is exactly what I intend to do. Humanity is in danger, and if we are to eliminate the threat, we must act with power and precision, as we did during the war. The Commonwealth may mean well, but they cannot possibly govern the fringes with wisdom from the safety of civilization. They cannot know the threats we are about to go up against, and if we deal with it effectively, they need never know how close they came to being subdued by the very evil they thought they defeated ten years ago.

"I, myself, cannot sit idly by and do nothing. And to follow the dictates of the Commonwealth at this point would be as good as doing nothing. Which is why I have severed communications with them."

It was credit to Ahab's reputation that none of the men shifted or batted an eye. He paused a moment as if to gauge their reactions, but they stood as immobile as statues.

"I recognize this may not have been what you signed up for. If there is uncertainty in your heart, then I have no desire to keep you here any more than you have to stay. Our courage cannot falter if we are to outwit our enemy. You have this one chance to leave. You will be set adrift in one of the life pods with a month's supply of rations. In all likelihood you'll be picked up within a week by the *Enderby*. Once you tell the Commonwealth of my decisions, you won't be charged for deserting your posts and should be able to find posts on any other ship."

Ahab paused again, as if expecting a mad dash for the life pod. Still no one moved. His eyebrows constricted into a fierce frown.

"I have no more to say on the matter. If you wish to go, you must go now. If you stay, I cannot promise death will spare you. I certainly will not flinch to put you in harm's way if that is what your duty requires."

Aside from the slight vibration of the engines, the ship remained completely silent. Nobody stirred.

Stubb cleared his throat. "Beggin' your pardon Captain, but I reckon the men'd like to return to their duties."

Ahab shot a sharp look at his second mate. Then understanding entered his eyes and he attempted to clear the emotion out of his throat. "Very well. We make for the planet of Good Hope. Tell your spotters to look sharp for Strags. Fifty credits for every sighting. Two hundred for every kill."

A cheer went up as Ahab left the bridge. But Starbuck remained as stern as ever, his presence returning calm and order where emotions threatened sloppy work. By evening the *Pequod* was functioning very much as it always had, but there was an eager alertness about the men that hadn't been there before.

Over the last few hours David had watched the men around him eagerly. He shared their anticipation, but not their experience. While the sailors around him settled quickly into expectations, his imagination fueled his agitated emotions. Ishmael took him in hand, helping the boy concentrate on the physical tasks at hand. Starbuck kept a watchful eye on the pair from above until the change of shifts.

David climbed into his hammock, weary with work and excitement. He just had enough time to wonder if his racing thoughts would keep him awake before his exhausted body took over and plunged him into a deep sleep.

Starbuck did not sleep well that night. He sat at his desk into the late hours, pouring over old files from the war, searching for evidence that would support his captain's quest. His left hand clutched a picture of his wife and son.

Back in New Bedford Harbor, the pub was filled to bursting with talk of the *Pequod* and its legendary Captain. Old salts from the war were pressed for tales of his early days on the outer edge, the great dangers of the wild nebulas, and the more recent tragedy when he had lost his beloved ship *Essex* and his leg all on one fateful voyage.

The grog flowed freely as the stories grew larger and larger, painting pictures of a Viking-like man with a leg fashioned out of the bones of his enemies, and a crew of invincible warriors. Finally, as the morning hours grew short and even the heartiest of drinkers began thinking thoughts of sleep, they raised a toast to the *Pequod*, captain, and crew, and speculated the daring stories it would bring back to harbor, all of them blissfully ignorant of the fateful events that had been set in motion.

♦ ♦ ♦

Ten days passed uneventfully. The crew worked as hard as ever, but the electric tension that had characterized them that first day seemed to have worn off. This was partly due to the familiarity of routine, and partly to the absence of Ahab on the bridge. He hadn't so much as shown his face since the first day of the voyage. When his mates entered his cabin to consult with him they found him studying his charts and notes obsessively. Starbuck took it upon himself to make sure Ahab was eating, carefully monitoring the cook's trays as they entered and exited the cabin.

With every passing day, David's nerves had faded and his confidence had grown. He was good natured, a quick study, and hard working. His fellow sailors didn't shy away from testing him on all three points and the mates watched shrewdly to see how he would fare. He passed with flying colors, putting so much diligence and effort into any task that was given to him that not even the crotchety old cook had a word to say against him. David soon began to wonder if his life before the *Pequod* had been real at all, or if perhaps he had only been sleeping. Something new awakened in him—something strong and bold and happy which had not been there previously.

As much as it pleased Starbuck, it also caused him a great deal of worry. He knew well the determination of Ahab. Whether they found the white MIC or not, this wasn't likely to be a routine voyage. It was one thing for the older sailors, many of whom were working off minor warrants, to accept the risks. But had they really given David a proper choice?

It wasn't natural for Starbuck to resent his captain and even the shadow of the temptation made him uncomfortable. Every night he became more sure that the evidence was against Ahab, and every day he became more convinced of what the truth would do to his captain. In his cabin he prayed passionately that the danger was not what Ahab believed. On the quarter deck he hoped that his captain would not be put to shame. Worst of all was the growing apprehension that these two goals were mutually exclusive.

Regardless of Starbuck's inward struggle, there was a ship to be run. Now, ten days into the voyage, the Helm was giving off increasingly anomalous energy readings. The First Mate took David and Ishmael and led the way through the maze of dripping coolant pipes, around the steaming ventilators, and down a slimy ladder to the lower engines. His boots landed in a thick, gooey substance, the color of cotton. Behind him, still descending the ladder, Ishmael gave a low whistle.

Starbuck scanned the chamber, his headlamp illuminating the darkness like the roving beam of a lighthouse. The light revealed strange starfish like creatures plastered to the walls.

"Clever little stowaways," Ishmael chuckled.

"Clever is right," Starbuck sighed good-naturedly. "I scanned the ship myself back in New Bedford."

"What are they, sir?" David asked.

"They're a type of barnacle," Starbuck replied. "They feed off engine radiation."

"But I thought engines didn't emit radiation anymore," David said.

Starbuck's light was sweeping up the walls now, surveying the extent of the infestation. The creatures glimmered pink and blue. "Radiation filters have proven a hundred percent effective on modern ships. But we had to adapt them to the *Pequod*'s engines. A small amount still leaks through."

"It don't hurt us none," Ishmael added, "but it's known to attract pesky buggers from time to time."

Starbuck smiled. "Pesky buggers, indeed."

"How do we get rid of them?" David asked.

"Well, in my day we used to find an able young lad to pick them off one by one and relocate them into the Soup," Ishmael said.

David's face contorted in dismay.

Starbuck gave a hearty laugh. "I do not think you are as old as that, Ishmael." He turned to David. "We can lure them out with an alternative source of radiation, but it will take twenty-four hours of drift. I'll alert the Captain."

The Gam Call sounded.

"Ship sighting!" Ishmael exclaimed with an eager grin.

But Starbuck's face darkened for a moment. Then he scurried back up the ladder and through the bowels of the ship with David and Ishmael close on his heels. On the main deck the crew was huddling around the one holo-pad, emptying their pockets and putting forth their best items to trade. Starbuck nimbly scaled the ladder to the quarter deck and proceeded confidently into the cabin. Ahab gave him a single glance before returning his attention to the holograph in front of him.

"I know the Strag yer talking about," the Captain of the other ship was saying. "Unnatural white with a twisted tail. Riddled with scars. Folks out here call it Moby Dick. We came across it two months ago. We were sittin' by a Red Dwarf, gutting a recent kill. It came out of nowhere and rammed us. My first mate was in a suit, overseeing the alloy harvesting. He was killed in seconds."

Ahab's brow darkened. "You have coordinates for me?"

"Sure, I can have them sent over, though I don't know that it'll be there anymore. What's this about, Captain Ahab? I never seen a Strag behave that way. Did the Commonwealth send you after it?"

"I'm not at liberty to discuss our commission at present," Ahab said tersely.

A cry went up suddenly from both crews. The other Captain smiled. "A spouting! I hope you do not expect me to give way to your seniority."

"Not at all," Ahab replied drily. "May the best ship take her first."

The ship's engines fired up again beneath them as the crew automatically prepared to make chase. The hologram flickered off and Ahab turned to Starbuck. "Set a new course with the coordinates provided."

Starbuck kept his hands behind his back and blinked. "Are we not to go after the Strag, sir?"

"I only have interest in one Strag, and we've just been given coordinates to its last known location."

Starbuck took a deep breath and pressed his lips together.

Ahab shifted. "If you have something to say, I'd rather you say it than give me your disapproving looks."

"It's just that a few hours' chase isn't likely to damage a trail that is already two months cold. And it may do a great deal to lift the men's spirits and ensure their future."

"We cannot think in terms of profit any longer, Starbuck. This is war."

"Even in war, men need to eat."

"Soldiering is a profession as much as sailing."

"Only if it is funded by a national treasury, and you yourself have said the Commonwealth does not back us." Starbuck swallowed. "Think how long it may yet be before you are proven right and the Commonwealth is on our side. Would it not be wise to ensure our venture is well-funded until then? We cannot know how long this hunt for Moby Dick will last."

Fire raged in Ahab's eyes and he struck the holographic console. Then his eyes cooled and he gave a long sigh. "You speak good sense, as usual. Lead the chase. I haven't the heart for it just now."

Starbuck nodded and turned to exit the cabin before the captain could change his mind.

"Starbuck," Ahab called after him.

Starbuck turned back apprehensively.

"Promise me you'll beat that crusty old codger to the prize."

The first mate forced a smile and left the cabin. He was pleased at the words that had come out of his mouth when a hundred harsher ones had simmered near the surface, and even more pleased that Ahab had listened to reason. Perhaps the Captain was not mad after all. There did, indeed, appear to be an unusual Strag wreaking havoc out here on the fringes. With everything Ahab had been through in the war, his emotional reaction to this Strag should not be surprising to Starbuck. He still had influence on the Captain and he would use it as much as he could to safeguard the future of the crew.

The ship was a flurry of excited activity when Starbuck stepped back onto the quarter deck. He called for reports.

"The *Jeroboam* is just outpacing us, sir. But the Strag's heading into an asteroid field."

"They've already marked their kill, sir," someone else said. "A flag just appeared on their hull."

Starbuck smiled. "The *Jeroboam* thinks we're old and slow. Shall we give them a surprise?"

A cheer went up from the crew.

"To the boats!" Starbuck called. "An extra portion of grog to the crew who delivers the killing blow!"

David and Ishmael followed Starbuck down the ladders to the lowest deck, where they piled into what appeared to be an oblong glass bubble. The hatch sealed over them as soon as all five men of Starbuck's crew were on board. Flask and Stubb each led their own crew into identical boats. Then the hull of the ship opened beneath them with a great shuddering.

One by one they dropped through and into open space. David gave a gasp as the boat bobbed and tipped like a gyroscope. The colors of the nebula swam all about them in great swathes of magenta and deep purple. Just ahead of them the first rocks of the asteroid field were coming into sight.

"The *Pequod* mayn't be as fast as the racy new vessels," Ishmael explained as his hands danced over the controls, "but her line of boats are still the fastest in the fleet. They stopped making 'em as they were too difficult to fly. Captain always makes sure we got the best pilots in the fleet." He winked.

"Less chatter, if you please." Starbuck sat in the stern, his eyes scanning the great digital navigation pad in front of him. "David, you'll assist Quinton on the starboard harpoon. Riggs and Melvin are on port. No fancy flying, Ishmael. I want a good, clean kill with no damage."

"Aye, sir."

The boat bobbed and weaved through the maze of asteroids with astounding speed. It soon became obvious they were gaining on the *Jeroboam*'s more traditional shuttles. Far ahead, the Strag began to grow in size.

Ishmael slid their boat under the belly of a large asteroid then banked steeply upwards to squeeze through the next gap. One of the *Jeroboam*'s shuttles, just ahead and off their starboard bow grazed an asteroid, sending the rock hurtling in their direction. Ishmael responded with lightning speed, sending their boat into a reverse spin that hurled them back and up.

Two asteroids collided just beneath them. They throttled forward again as a chain reaction of debris spread out behind them. Starbuck quickly checked his charts to make sure Stubb and Flask weren't caught in the wake. The damaged *Jeroboam* shuttle peeled off and slowly reversed course.

"They look as though they mean to continue the hunt with only two shuttles," David cried out in surprise.

"It can be done," Starbuck replied calmly. "The profit would offset the cost of damages they just incurred."

But all three *Pequod* boats were clearly outstripping the *Jeroboam* shuttles now.

"We're coming up port-side, sir," Ishmael said. "Be in range in about twenty seconds."

"Take the starboard flank, Stubb," Starbuck ordered through his communicator. "Hang back for a moment Flask and watch the Strag's first flounder, then move in as you see fit."

"Aye, aye, sir!"

Stubb's boat moved into place swiftly, and seconds later a harpoon shot off, burrowing into the Strag's hull. The Strag whipped its tail and swerved left. Quinton fired off a second harpoon from Starbuck's boat. It also hit its target. Ishmael pulled the boat into reverse. It lurched from the sudden tension on the cable. The Strag was dragging them now and it was all Ishmael could do to keep from bumping into the nearby asteroids.

"It's not slowing down!" David exclaimed.

"It will," Starbuck said.

The Strag swerved left and right, trying to run them into the asteroids. Flask's boat maneuvered overhead, shooting a third harpoon into the Strag. Now it began to buck wildly, but its speed was noticeably decreasing.

"Time to get to work," Starbuck spoke to all three boats through the communicator. "Let's finish this before this thing hurls us into an asteroid."

Flask shot a lance, but the trajectory was off and it glanced off the Strag's hull. Quinton's lance, however, managed to pierce the Strag's stern hull, leaking a red fluid. It washed over their boat in little rivulets. It was Stubb's lance that finally struck deep enough to disable the motherboard.

The Strag rolled and writhed as its systems sizzled out. All three boats severed their harpoons and rolled out of range of the dying Strag. It bled out in front of them, green and blue fluid now mixing with the red, creating a rainbow aurora that was somehow melancholy in its beauty. The Strag went still, the aurora of its fluids expanding to envelop them. There was a minute of silence when nobody spoke.

"Stubb, I believe you have earned the right to tow our prize back to the *Pequod*," Starbuck said.

"Permission to take a low pass over the *Jerry*, sir?"

Several of the crew chuckled.

"Permission denied," Starbuck replied evenly. "They can see us just as well if we take a straight path. Their egos are already bruised. No need to create ill will."

"Aye, sir. We'll be as dignified as angels."

Stubb's boat began to maneuver the Strag up out of the asteroid field.

"Keep on their flank, Ishmael, in case they run into any trouble."

"Aye, sir."

Their boat rolled upward at a reduced speed, gracefully dodging the asteroids until they popped back out into open space. David finally relaxed in his chair. He had forgotten which way was up and down and didn't much care anymore. His muscles were aching from the effort. Now he almost felt weightless, as if he were free floating in a suit. His eyes remained locked on the bleeding Strag dragging on the end of Stubb's cable.

"It sure is something, isn't it?" Ishmael chuckled. "The only thing those clankers are good for is the light show they put on when they're dead."

Starbuck didn't answer, but his mouth tightened.

The three boats slipped back into the belly of the *Pequod*, their new prize now tethered to the bowsprit. They were greeted by the remaining crew, who hauled them up out of the boats and slapped them on the back.

Knowing his captain's eagerness to get moving, Starbuck quickly made his way back to the main deck to supervise the harvesting of the MIC. He grabbed his suit as soon as he hit main deck and began assembling his team when the captain's voice sounded from the quarter deck.

"All hands avast!"

Starbuck turned in surprise. Ahab himself was descending the ladder in a salvage suit. Two strange men followed behind him. Their heads were shaved and their foreheads were marked with identical tattoos. The sign of the Metal Worshippers. The ship grew deathly quiet.

"I'll oversee the harvest myself," Ahab said evenly, not seeming to have noticed the change in the crew.

"Of course, Captain." Starbuck's voice was calm but he eyed the men coldly. "Permission to join you, sir."

The crew waited with baited breath, watching their captain and first mate as if their lives depended on it.

"There's no need for that," Ahab replied casually. "I'll call you if I want you." He led the two men confidently across the frozen ship to the starboard bow hatch.

Starbuck followed on his heels, keeping his voice calm. "It's just I forgot to mention we discovered barnacles in the lower engine room just before our encounter with the *Jeroboam*."

All four men stepped into the airlock and out of earshot of the crew. Ahab's two men began donning their helmets.

"Are you really bothering me about barnacles?" Ahab asked.

"May I have a word with you, sir?" Starbuck asked forcefully.

Ahab sighed, signaled to his two men to wait, then stepped aside with Starbuck.

"Do you really think it wise to have Metal Worshippers on this ship?" Starbuck asked in a fierce whisper.

"I did not tell you because I knew you would not approve—"

"*I* would not approve?" Starbuck asked. "You hate them more than anyone! I've heard you say it!"

"I did not say I invited them on board to have tea," Ahab replied sharply. His eyes glinted.

"But you trust them enough to take them with you? To reunite them with one of the most venerated objects of their twisted religion?"

"I did not say I trust them either. Would you kindly stop dictating my intentions."

"What are your intentions?" Starbuck crossed his arms.

"To stop a war," Ahab replied.

"By enlisting the humans who turned on their own kind during the last one?" Starbuck hissed.

"Do you really know anything about that creature out there?" Ahab asked. "Do any of us? Too much knowledge nearly destroyed humanity, but ignorance is threatening to cripple us. These men know how the MICs work."

"And you expect them to help you?" Starbuck asked.

A strange look came over Ahab's face. "I do."

"Care to tell me why?"

Ahab narrowed his eyes. "A few weeks ago you said you'd follow me to the end of the world. Are you taking those words back now?"

"Is this the end of the world, then?" Starbucks asked softly.

"It might be."

"Is that why you're willing to dance with the devil?" Starbuck asked.

"Starbuck, I know the stakes, I know the enemy, and I know what it's going to take to defeat him. I will not apologize for what I have to do. If it makes you uncomfortable, you had better leave sooner than later."

"Do you want me to leave?"

"No. I want you by my side. You have always made me stronger."

"You must know that I do not question you out of disloyalty. I question you in private so that I can support you in front of the crew."

"I am not threatened by your questions. I never have been. But you are a better man than I, and I would not be offended should you decide to sit this one out. I give you the same offer I gave every man on this ship the day we departed."

"Would you stop trying to get rid of your friends?"

The corner of Ahab's mouth turned up.

"Do I think it foolhardy to take two Metal Worshipers onto a MIC? Yes. Do you know better than I? Perhaps you do. In the end, it matters little to me whether I am right or wrong so long as I am by your side to help you bear it. Let me come with you on this harvest so that you may at least have one arm you may depend upon."

Ahab grasped the side of his friend's face. "Somehow, I suspect if I gave a hundred legs for you in a hundred lifetimes, I would still fall short of deserving your unwavering friendship."

Starbuck laughed. "That's nonsense, and it's exactly why I had better come along—to make sure you don't throw your one life away recklessly."

Ahab smiled.

Starbuck ducked back into the main cabin to advise Stubb. But he was back and in his suit in a flash. The two Metal Worshippers stared at him as stoically as if they didn't know the extended argument they had just witnessed had been about them. Starbuck met their gaze boldly though it sent a chill down his spine.

Ahab depressurized the airlock then led the way, stepping out into the Soup. The two Metal Worshippers followed him. Starbuck did a quick check on all the harnesses before stepping out himself.

Starbuck never felt quite comfortable in null gravity, though as with most challenges in his life he had learned to cope admirably. On the other hand, Ahab's steadfast confidence seemed amplified in open space, almost as if without the confines of his ship another nature took over. He glided towards the Strag carcass, his muscles coiled to spring in any direction.

A few seconds later he landed lightly on the hull of the Strag, sliding nimbly up over its belly to the vulnerably point just below its chin. He had pulled out his torch and deftly cut an entry by the time the Metal Worshippers and Starbuck caught up with him. Ahab slipped through the hole into the guts of the Strag. The other three followed after, reorienting themselves and activating their magnetic boots.

The interior was dark and claustrophobic. Massive clusters of circuits and wires hung from the skeletal frame like large muscle groups and organs, leaving very little room for a grown man to move around. Ahab narrowed his eyes, expecting any moment for a ligament to break free and wrap around his neck.

Ahab turned to one of the Metal Worshippers. "Fedallah, you said you can pull data off the memory drive?"

"I'll do my best," Fedallah said. "It depends on how much damage your lances did. Elijah will show you the command matrix."

"Starbuck, I reckon you'd like to join Fedallah?" There was amusement in Ahab's eyes.

Starbuck nodded.

"Then let's get moving."

Starbuck followed his guide through the maze of tangled wires, back towards the dorsal fin. Fedallah stooped, carefully brushing wires aside to reveal an access panel. He pulled a small tool off his belt and began loosening the panel.

"I don't need to watch my back around you, do I?" he asked.

"You are under the protection of the Captain," Starbuck said. "No harm will come to you by my hand...unless you put him in danger."

"You are very loyal to your captain," Fedallah said with a smirk.

"Why does he trust you?"

Fedallah pried back the panel, revealing a complex circuit board of blinking lights, which meant absolutely nothing to Starbuck. "I thought he explained it to you back on the ship."

"I would like to hear your understanding of the terms of your agreement."

Fedallah chuckled. "He didn't tell you. Well, I never made any promises to withhold information from you. What is meant to be will come to pass."

"What does that mean?" Starbuck frowned.

"Let me show you," Fedallah said. He pulled out a digital interface, connected it to the circuit board and punched a series of buttons. Symbols began to scroll across the screen. Fedallah held it up for Starbuck to see.

"Is that supposed to mean something to me?"

"This is the language of the machines," Fedallah explained. "You destroyed their ability to communicate across subspace, but they can still pass messages on contact."

"Impossible," Starbuck interrupted. "They don't have the capacity for that."

"That's what the Commonwealth would like to believe," Fedallah replied. "The machines evolved intelligence once, what makes you think they could not do it again? It is their destiny." Fedallah's eyes glowed.

Starbuck swallowed. "I don't believe in destiny."

Fedallah smiled, an eerie glow from the circuit panels lighting up his face. "Screws and bolts do not pretend to be free agents. It is the weakness of humans to believe in free will. But by its nature, the entire universe is a machine."

"So why are you helping Captain Ahab? Because you believe that ultimately he can't do anything to stop the MICs?"

Fedallah typed a command into his digital interface and held it up. "Your captain wants to find a certain MIC, and it seems a certain MIC wants to find him. It is his destiny."

The symbols on the screen changed suddenly into numbers and letters. Starbuck could recognize many of the words, though they didn't make sense in context. But interspersed between the strange combinations of words, punctuation, and numbers, one name repeated over and over: Ahab.

Starbuck's heart froze and the blood drained from his face. Just then Ahab and Elijah reappeared.

"Have you got what you need?" Ahab asked.

"Aye, sir." Fedallah held up his digital interface in demonstration.

"I assume you two would prefer not to witness the harvest?" Ahab asked.

"It would be offensive to us," Elijah said.

Ahab nodded. "We will return to the *Pequod*." His eyes shifted to Starbuck. "I'll send a team back over to assist you."

"Captain," Starbuck stepped forward, "perhaps now would be a good time to purge those barnacles, while we're harvesting."

Ahab's eyes narrowed.

Fedallah stepped closer to him. "You will need your engines at peak efficiency to catch the White MIC."

Ahab nodded. "I should also like to see the smith about a harpoon."

"The *Pequod* has plenty of harpoons," Starbuck said.

"This one shall be fashioned from the bones of the *Essex*," Ahab's eyes glinted, "and when it sinks into Moby Dick's hull, that white demon will feel the sting of every life it's taken."

Fedallah and Elijah exchanged glances.

Starbuck gritted his teeth, but he said nothing. Ahab and the two Metal Worshippers returned to the ship and a proper harvesting crew floated over to assist Starbuck. Yet even as he supervised dutifully, the first mate's thoughts were far away. The small space filled with light and heat as the harvesters systematically broke down the precious alloys into raw liquid. As soon as the barrels were full burly crew members sent them floating back to the *Pequod*. They ripped the cables and wiring out of the bulwarks and fed them through a differentiator. From stem to stern, they ripped and gutted the MIC of crystals and alloys. The dross burned up in green flames, filling the small space with noxious fumes.

If Starbuck had ever enjoyed the harvesting process, it was on account of the men. A harvest always meant profit. The men usually laughed and joked as they melted, hacked, and sawed their livelihood out of the flesh of the dead machine. Tonight they were quiet, sullen, and nervous. The prize in front of them couldn't entirely blot out the recent strange turn of events. It was no secret that Captain Ahab often charted his course off the map, but working with Metal Worshippers was another thing entirely.

Starbuck's reaction had gone a long way to spread calm. He was the emotional weather gauge for the crew. No storm would hit them without passing through him first. Still, there were no jokes during harvest this time. Perhaps that was why Starbuck noticed for the first time how eerie everything looked. The green light and foul smoke turned even the most familiar faces into ghosts. Perhaps that was all they were— a ghost ship full of ghost men. No man had chosen their fate—not even Ahab. There were forces at work bigger than all of them. Starbuck could not claim to understand them, but for the sake of the crew he vowed to navigate them as competently as he did the stars, or die trying.

ABOUT THE AUTHOR

E.B. Dawson was born out of time. Raised in the remote regions of a developing nation, traveling to America was as good as traveling thirty years into the future. Now she writes science fiction and fantasy to make sense of her unusual perspectives on life. Her stories acknowledge darkness, but empower and encourage people to keep on fighting, no matter how difficult their circumstances may be.

OTHER WORKS BY E.B. DAWSON

The Creation of Jack Series
- Out of Darkness
- Into the Void
- Under the Skin
- Until the End

The Lost Empire Series
- The Traveler
- The Citizen

Short Stories
- Striker (available in the Phoenix Fiction Writers Anthology: *Antiheroes)*